ANNABELLE SAMI ILLUSTRATED BY DANIELA SOSA

Agent Zaiba
INVESTIGATES

THE SMUGGLER'S SECRET

LITTLE TIGER
LONDON

I

SECRETS OF THE PAST

"Zaiba! Look!"

"I can't talk right now, Poppy. I'm on the verge of a great discovery!" Zaiba kept her gaze firmly fixed on the pieces of broken pottery in front of her as she searched for the last piece. As a successful detective, she knew it was important to be patient and methodical.

"But Zaiba – look at this." Poppy held up a cape of rainbow colours. "I've finished!"

Zaiba turned to her best friend who was sitting at the table next to her. The two of them were in their classroom, though it was now well after school hours. They were at their new favourite after-school activity: History Club!

Every member of the club had been given a project, to recreate something from the past. Poppy had chosen the history of fashion and immediately set to the task, channelling her love of clothes. She'd reworked some old items from her wardrobe into a ninteen-seventies rock-star cape with big, multicoloured stripes and a high, sequinned collar. It looked spot on!

Zaiba was very impressed. With all the sequins and Lycra, it had taken Poppy ages to transform her old clothes into something worthy of a rock star.

"Wow, Poppy! You're a genius. How did you make that?"

"Lots of hard work … and watching YouTube videos of some old TV show called *Top of the Pops*." Poppy's face gleamed with pride. "I had to get the style exactly right. It's called glam rock. All the glam rock stars in the 1970s had big hair, platform shoes and these bright costumes. I wish I could wear it, but it's a little small for me. I need a shorter model…" Poppy glanced hopefully at Zaiba's younger brother Ali who was sitting across from her at a large desk, studying a massive book with dusty pages. "Ali?" She held up the cape, glittering with sequins.

"I really think this would suit you."

Ali didn't even look up. "Not likely."

Zaiba and Poppy laughed. One of the benefits of the younger years being allowed to join History Club was that they could occasionally tease Ali! And as their teacher Ms Talbot said, "People of all ages can appreciate the past!"

Poppy peered at Zaiba's project. While Ali had chosen to study Ada Lovelace – "Basically the first computer programmer!" – Zaiba had chosen ... teapots.

She scratched her head. "Remind me again why you picked this for your project, Zai."

"Aunt Fouzia has an amazing collection of antique teapots. You know she loves her chai!" Zaiba explained, sorting through the pieces of pottery. "She has ones from Pakistan, China and India. Tea has such an interesting history – tied in with so many different historical events. Did you know that the East India Trading Company exported its first order of tea to the UK in 1664? I found out about the company when I was doing my research. They were also responsible for a lot of looting, slavery

3

and violence across India and beyond. That's why it's important to read history from lots of different sources. Like when we talk to lots of different leads investigating a crime!" Poppy was an excellent detective's assistant.

"That is interesting," Poppy agreed. "Who knew teapots could lead to you learning all that?"

Zaiba nodded and went back to fiddling with the fragments of pottery that she'd glued back together. They were reddish-brown and had a logo stamped into the base, but Zaiba couldn't work out what it said until she found the last piece to fit the gap.

Poppy watched as Zaiba sorted through endless small shards of red ceramics until...

"There!" Zaiba beamed as she turned a small piece over and slid it into place. "Now I can finally see the logo."

It was a large, curly 'A' with the words *Admaston, 1820* underneath.

"Wow!" Zaiba breathed. "You can learn a lot from a logo. Admaston must be the place where this teapot was made all those years ago."

"Zaiba! Check this out!" a voice called from the other

side of the classroom.

It was Zaiba's cousin Mariam. Zaiba and Mariam hadn't always got on so well, but since Mariam had helped Zaiba and her team — officially known as the Snow Leopard Detective Agency — solve a mysterious poisoning case at their school summer fete, they'd become friends.

Mariam had chosen to work on filling out a family tree that already stretched back generations! But before Zaiba could check out her cousin's latest family discovery, Ms Talbot's voice rang out. "Fellow historians! Gather round! Do you remember I told you that an old sunken shipwreck was discovered off Chesil Bay on the south coast?"

There was excited chatter from the History Club as everyone gathered to sit on the carpet.

Ms Talbot paused to clear her throat. "I have some exciting news. The headteacher has agreed..." Ms Talbot left a short pause. Zaiba could hardly bear it any longer, the suspense was too much! "... that the History Club can take an expedition to Chesil Bay — next weekend!"

The class cheered and some of them even leaped to their feet!

"And there's more!" Ms Talbot glanced around, her face flushed with excitement. "Yesterday, divers recovered a priceless artefact from the wreckage! Its identity is being kept secret because it's so valuable. All we know is that the artefact originates from the Assam region of India." Her face turned serious. "Of course, it's important to return historical items to their place of origin ... which is why this item will be returned to its rightful home very soon."

Zaiba raised her hand and wiggled it in her teacher's direction.

"Yes, Zaiba?"

"Where is the artefact now?" she asked. As a detective it was always important to gather all known information about a mystery – and the unnamed artefact was certainly mysterious.

Ms Talbot smiled. "It's being kept safely at a local museum in Chesil Bay until it's returned to India. But the museum is going to have a big reveal of what it is on Sunday – and the History Club are invited!"

Cheers rang out! This is what they'd all been waiting

for – to be some of the first people to lay eyes on a real-life detail from history.

"We still need to secure a couple of chaperones but I'm sure that won't be a problem." Ms Talbot's eyes glinted. "I'm also *very* excited that we will be going on a glass-bottom boat trip to see the shipwreck up close ourselves. So, fellow historians, I set you this challenge." Ms Talbot raised a finger in the air. "Who can discover what the mystery artefact is before the reveal on Sunday?"

Zaiba smiled and squeezed her hands together. Uncovering a mystery was the perfect challenge for her!

Dinnertime was abuzz with talk of the class trip.

"So, our mission is to find out what the mystery artefact is. *And* we get to go on a glass-bottom boat to look at the shipwreck – so I'm sure I'll find some clues there!" Zaiba mumbled through a mouth full of keema naan.

"That's very exciting, honey," said Jessica, Zaiba's

stepmum, pointing to her own mouth. "But I don't need to see your dinner."

Zaiba wiped the grease from her face with a unicorn-print paper napkin. "I'm sorry." She'd always been told how important it was to be polite at the table, but the lamb and onion filling was delicious! "It's just so exciting!"

A priceless artefact surely meant that crime could be just around the corner. Zaiba secretly imagined what it would be like if she personally was asked to guard the artefact. An agent's job was varied – who knew what might happen?

"So, is this the Snow Leopard Detective Agency's latest case?" Zaiba's dad Hassan asked, looking from Zaiba to Ali. They nodded furiously.

"I can't wait!" Ali announced happily. "Chesil Bay is on the Jurassic coast, which gets its name because of all the fossils there! I wonder how old the rock formations are…"

Zaiba could see the cogs in Ali's head whirring, as he got ready to absorb lots of facts about fossils.

"Wait a minute," Hassan asked. "What's the name of the town again?"

"Chesil Bay," said Ali.

Hassan's face lit up! "Chesil Bay? That's where the famous cricket club is, isn't it?" He carried on talking without waiting for a reply. "The third oldest in the country. Queen Victoria even visited it in 1870! I'd love to go there myself..." He looked suddenly hopeful and leaned across the dining table. "Did your teacher mention anything about needing chaperones?"

"Yes!" Zaiba said. "Ms Talbot said for parents to ring if they were interested in coming." She went to her backpack where she'd carefully kept the permission slips for both her and Ali. She slid them across the table.

The History Club Outing to Chesil Bay

Conducted by Ms Loretta Talbot

Your child/ren is/are cordially invited to a historical exploration of beautiful Chesil Bay. We will be staying at Chalk Cottage — a safe and highly recommended B&B in the town (please see the website for details).

Please pack:

- summer clothes

- swimwear

- sensible shoes for walking

- overnight clothes

- toiletries

An anorak or windbreaker for our boat tour of the sunken shipwreck is advisable.

Parent chaperones needed! Please ring the number at the bottom of this form if interested.

"Well!" Jessica announced, looking fondly at Zaiba, Ali and Hassan. "I think I'd better ask to come too. None of us wants to miss out on a family trip!" She glanced around again. "Right?"

Everyone gave a big thumbs up. Then Zaiba's dad snatched up the form and immediately slipped into the other room, abandoning his meal – a big deal for Hassan! Zaiba could tell he was going to call Ms Talbot. She'd noticed him pop his phone in his pocket on the way out. A good detective caught even the smallest of details, which reminded Zaiba … she'd promised to video call her Aunt Fouzia that evening.

Aunt Fouzia was the sister of Zaiba's birth mum, who Zaiba called Ammi. Her aunt also happened to be the best detective in the whole of Pakistan! The two sisters had set up the world-renowned Snow Leopard Detective Agency before Zaiba was born. Zaiba's ammi had gone missing on a mission when Zaiba was just a baby and she missed her a lot. But having an auntie as brilliant as Fouzia meant she still felt a connection to her mum.

"Come on, Ali," Zaiba said, quickly popping a last piece of garlic-roasted broccoli into her mouth. Yum! "We need to see what Aunt Fouzia has to say about priceless artefacts."

The two of them went to snuggle up together on the sofa, with a soft blanket that covered both their knees. They reached to open the family laptop. Aunt Fouzia's face popped up on the screen instantly!

"Auntie!" Zaiba and Ali cried, each of them jostling to get in shot. Aunt Fouzia was a short lady with thick black hair, just like Zaiba's. Her smile was as wide as ever but there were bags under her eyes and Zaiba could detect a slight sag in her shoulders. Her auntie was tired.

"My sweeties!" Aunt Fouzia said. "You called at the perfect time. Samirah will be here to say hello soon. Ah, here she is!"

Zaiba smiled as her cousin walked into view, carrying a little bundle with a tuft of brown hair poking out the top. Sam, Aunt Fouzia's daughter, had just had a baby. She was named Nabiha, after Zaiba's ammi. Without a shadow of a doubt, she was the cutest baby ever!

Behind her cousin and aunt, Zaiba noticed that the living-room floor was strewn with baby blankets, toys and picture books. So that's why Aunt Fouzia looked tired! It seemed like looking after a baby was a lot of work.

Zaiba wondered if her ammi had been just as tired looking after her. She had lots of questions she wished she could ask her. She did have the notes that her mum had scribbled in Zaiba's treasured Eden Lockett novels, though. These little notes had helped her solve many mysteries in her life – not just the detective ones.

"I want to hear all about your latest adventures." Aunt Fouzia waved her hand at the screen. "Tell me everything."

While Samirah breastfed Nabiha in the background, Ali and Zaiba filled in their aunt on all their History Club projects, finishing with details about their upcoming trip to Chesil Bay.

Aunt Fouzia smiled. Her eyes had a dreamy look. "I'm a little jealous. A sunken shipwreck? That sounds very exciting!"

Zaiba gasped. "But Auntie, you're the best detective

in the whole of Pakistan. You must be on thrilling cases all the time!"

Her aunt rocked on the Bokhara mat, where she was sat cross-legged. "Ha! It's true! I've had a wonderful career. And I'm a nanny now, which is also a very important job. I have to use my detective skills to work out why the baby's crying, when Samirah needs to rest and – most importantly – when Nabiha's nappy needs changing." She took the baby from Samirah and lifted her bum up to her nose, inhaling deeply.

"Ah, yes!" she cried. "I detect that this nappy needed changing at least – let me think – eight minutes ago."

"Ewwww!" Zaiba and Ali screwed up their noses. Nabiha was very cute, but they weren't too keen on changing nappies.

Samirah buttoned up her blouse and waved to Zaiba and Ali. "Thank you, Mum. Now if you'll excuse me..." She took her baby back into her arms and carried her into another room.

Suddenly, Aunt Fouzia's face lit up. "I must show you the new project I'm working on! Let me go and fetch it."

Zaiba's eyes grew wide with anticipation. What could it be? A thrilling new international crime to solve? A global gang Aunt Fouzia was about to bust?

Her aunt popped back into the frame, carrying a large book. "It's a scrapbook!" Aunt Fouzia beamed. She began flicking through the pages, which had old photos and newspaper clippings pasted to them. "I call it my 'Scrapbook of Legends'. It's to keep track of my career and the interesting people I've worked with. These agents have mostly retired but I still keep their names confidential." She tapped the side of her nose, as she always did when something was a secret. Zaiba had taken to copying the trait sometimes when she wanted to be mysterious. "For example, this woman..." Aunt Fouzia pointed to someone wearing a fedora. "She had the best sense of smell in Pakistan. Very useful."

She pointed to another photo. "And this man... I'll always remember the little snort he did when he laughed! Ah, what wonderful memories." Aunt Fouzia turned the scrapbook round and began to flick through the pages with a fond look on her face.

Zaiba realized that the scrapbook was Aunt Fouzia's very own personal history project – an important history of detecting in Pakistan. The people in the snapshots were legends in their lifetimes. And, Zaiba also realized ... she could be one too!

Aunt Fouzia had put her in charge of the UK branch of the Snow Leopard Detective Agency. With the help of Poppy and Ali, Zaiba had solved three cases already. Who knew? If they were to solve more crimes, perhaps one day she would be added to the Scrapbook of Legends? It was more than she dared to dream!

They'd barely said their goodbyes and closed the laptop when Hassan burst into the room, his face alight. Jessica was right behind him, looking almost as giddy. "Attention, everyone!" he announced. "You'll be glad to hear that Ms Talbot has decreed we shall *all* be visiting Chesil Bay next weekend!"

The family erupted in cheers. Zaiba was on the scent of a mystery and her family were coming with her – she couldn't wait!

2
JOURNEY TO CHESIL BAY

"This is the 15:45 service to Whistchurch calling at Herrington, Kilton, Chesil Bay..." The automatic announcement came over the platform speakers.

"That's our train, everyone. Get ready!" Ms Talbot flapped, trying to organize the group into a line.

The History Club boarded the carriage with their luggage. Zaiba, Poppy, Ali and Mariam quickly found themselves a table seat and settled down. Wheels rumbled as they pulled out of the station. Zaiba took a picture of them sitting at their seats, waving, and sent it to Aunt Fouzia.

We're off! Will let you know when we arrive. xx

Zaiba gazed out at the scenery as it sped past the window. She felt a flutter of excitement in her stomach. Going to a totally new place was always exciting. But going to a new place to see a sunken shipwreck and uncover the identity of a priceless historical artefact? That was totally flutter-worthy!

The carriage was filled with excited voices, plus the munching of snacks and the occasional *shhh*! from Ms Talbot. Hassan and Jessica had sat a little way down the aisle to give Zaiba and Ali some freedom.

Mariam was dishing out playing cards that Aunt Raim had given her for the journey. Zaiba thought about how much her relationship with her cousin had changed in the last year. She and Mariam had been rivals since childhood, with Mariam often getting in the way of Zaiba's investigations and taking any opportunity to tell on her. Now they were firm friends, and Mariam was an honorary member of the Snow Leopard Detective Agency!

"Snap!" Poppy shouted.

Ms Talbot turned round in her seat. "I know you're having fun, but you must remember we aren't the only passengers on the train."

Ms Talbot was right. Zaiba had been so excited about the journey that she'd forgotten to do her observations!

"Poppy," she whispered. "Quick observations of the carriage – see anything suspicious?"

They glanced around. There was a young couple sitting at the back of the carriage, whispering and making smoochy faces at one another. Zaiba and Poppy looked at each other and screwed up their noses.

"What about that guy?" Ali pointed across the aisle.

"Don't point, Ali – it's rude!" Mariam pushed his hand down.

"And it draws attention to us." Zaiba followed Ali's gaze to an elderly gentleman, sitting by himself. He was fumbling with the latch of a shiny leather briefcase. The train bumped on the rails and he lost his grip, the case falling to the floor.

"What's that?" Zaiba said, noticing an object tumble out. The older man picked it up quickly and stuffed it back in his case but not before Zaiba had caught a glimpse of it. "A magnifying glass?"

"Like the ones Sherlock Holmes used?" Ali asked, quieter this time.

"What could he need that for?" Zaiba pondered.

"Maybe he's trying to find out what the artefact is – just like us!" Poppy suggested.

"Maybe," Zaiba said. "Talking of the artefact... We know it's from Assam, but I wish we had a few more clues about its identity." She couldn't help feeling a bit impatient!

"I bet it's a case of silk dresses..." Poppy's eyes took on a dreamy look.

"*As if*. It won't be something silly like dresses." Mariam rolled her eyes. "I bet it's scrolls with important writing on!"

Zaiba sighed. Mariam was definitely nicer but she could still be a bit blunt at times.

Ali shook his head. "It'll be something made of sturdy but precious material. That'll be why they don't want to reveal its identity straight away. Maybe it's ... gold! Did you know that gold is non-reactive, so it doesn't rust, no matter how old it is?"

Ali was a fact master, so Zaiba always trusted his information. Perhaps the artefact *was* gold... Zaiba's head was abuzz with the possibilities. But she knew that wild guesses would get them nowhere. A good detective examined the clues and came to a conclusion. Zaiba patted her backpack and felt the copy of the Eden Lockett book she had brought on the trip. Zaiba had decided to bring *The Cottage on the Cliff* with her for inspiration, as it was set at the seaside too.

Eden Lockett was a fictional detective but she was based on a real person. The author used a pen name to protect her identity because – as Aunt Fouzia always said – some things are on a need-to-know basis.

A flash of blue in the corner of her eye caught Zaiba's attention. Her head snapped round and she pushed her nose to the train window. Outside was a huge expanse of blue and a rocky coastline, with seagulls floating in the air. Her friends scrambled to the window and peered out beside her.

"Detectives," Zaiba said as she listed items on her

fingers. "What do sand, seagulls and fish and chips all have in common?" She turned to see their eager faces staring out of the window.

The voices of the UK branch of the Snow Leopard Detective Agency rang out with the perfect answer. "THE SEASIDE!"

The first thing Zaiba noticed when they hopped out of the bus from the station was a delicious aroma. Tangy, spicy and fragrant. Eden Lockett's golden rule number four stated: *Use every sense available to you. Touch, sound, taste, smell and sight.*

Zaiba decided to do just that.

"We have arrived at the B&B in Chesil Bay. Time is..." She checked her mobile phone. "17:30 hours. This is Agent Zaiba. Observations are as follows. I can feel a gravel pathway beneath my feet. I hear seagulls calling, and waves! And lots of chattering from my group. I can taste a little salt from the sea in the air. I can smell—"

"The most delicious curry ever!" Ali butted in.

Zaiba cleared her throat. "And to conclude the observations, ahead of us I can see a white stone building – two storeys – on the clifftop. Surrounded by grass and other buildings. More observations to come."

Zaiba clicked off the recorder as a friendly looking couple walked down the path.

"Welcome to Chesil Bay and Chalk Cottage," the woman said, opening her arms. "I'm Khushi."

"And I'm Anil Dutta," the man added. "We're so happy to have you to stay. Please follow us inside."

The group hurried after them, lugging their overnight bags. They congregated in the lobby while Ms Talbot sorted out room assignments. Zaiba had overheard a lot of her classmates talking excitedly about the rooms as this was their first holiday away from their parents. Speaking of which... Zaiba spotted her own parents talking to the Duttas over by reception. She grabbed Poppy, who had been admiring the lobby's decor, and pulled her over to the desk.

"Ah, this is my daughter Zaiba and her friend Poppy," Hassan said, patting them both fondly on the head.

Zaiba wished he wouldn't do that – she was a fully-fledged detective, after all!

Anil and Khushi smiled warmly down at them.

"I'm Ali!" announced Zaiba's brother, wriggling through everyone.

"Nice to meet you, Ali," Khushi said.

"I was wondering... What is that smell? It's delicious!" he exclaimed.

Anil grinned. "That's my famous masor tenga," he explained. "It's a traditional fish curry from Assam, where my wife and I are originally from."

The same place as the artefact! Zaiba thought. She made a mental note to ask the Duttas later about Assam. This was her first lead!

"I always make masor tenga when my friends are coming over to watch the cricket," Anil added.

Hassan gasped. "Of course, the cricket's on tonight! I think Pakistan are playing India?" Zaiba was impressed that he *almost* managed to make it sound as though he had only just remembered.

"You're welcome to join us," Anil said, with an

understanding smile.

"But only after your chaperoning duties are finished, of course." Zaiba poked her dad in his tummy, teasing him.

"I'd be delighted to join you," Hassan told Anil. "Though you should know, I will be supporting Pakistan." Zaiba smiled at her dad puffing out his chest with pride for his home country.

Anil looked ready to launch into some friendly banter but Ms Talbot had walked over, reading from a list. "Zaiba, Poppy, Ali and Mariam ... you're in room six, with the bunk beds."

"Bagsy top bunk!" Mariam cried, grabbing the room key. She raced up the winding stairs. Zaiba, Poppy and Ali collected their bags and set off behind her.

"Be careful!" Jessica called after them, but they had already disappeared up the wooden staircase and along a narrow, carpeted corridor to where Mariam was fumbling with the room key.

"All right, Mariam, you won the top bunk," Zaiba conceded, dragging her overnight case behind her.

"No fair, she got a head start!" Ali grumbled.

Poppy and Zaiba shared a look and nodded in understanding. Now wasn't the time to fight over beds.

"Ali, you can have the other top bunk," Zaiba said.

Ali punched his hand in the air. "Yes!"

The door swung open and they stepped into a room that was big enough to fit two bunk beds against each wall. A large window looked out over the ocean and they could see all the way to the horizon.

What a view!

Zaiba slid out her copy of *The Cottage on the Cliff*. It fell open on a page that Zaiba had bookmarked. It was the point in the story when Eden had arrived at the cottage and was busy scribbling down a floorplan. Zaiba suddenly felt a pang of guilt – should she be doing the same, rather than messing about with her friends? But then she noticed what her ammi had written in the margin: *All work and no play makes a boring detective!*

Zaiba giggled, which caught Poppy's attention. She showed Poppy the note and it made her laugh too.

"Your ammi is right. Fun is important. And so is food!" Zaiba heard Poppy's tummy rumble, as though to emphasize her point.

"Ms Talbot said to meet downstairs for dinner at six," Mariam called from the top bunk. "We should go down before Poppy's stomach complains again!"

Zaiba totally agreed. "Agents assemble," she announced. "For food!"

3
SETTING SAIL

"Whoa, whoa, WHOA!"

The water was choppy and the morning air fresh, as the History Club boarded the glass-bottom boat the next day. Poppy clung to Zaiba's hand as she climbed on, wobbling as she went. She was wearing her favourite jellies but they clearly didn't have enough grip. Everyone was wearing neon-yellow life jackets, which Poppy had described as a "fashion disaster!" but Zaiba didn't care. It meant they were all safe.

Waves splashed against the hull of the boat tied up in the small harbour. It wasn't the huge craft Zaiba had imagined it would be but it was big enough for the whole

History Club, plus a handful of other tourists.

They all quietened down to listen to a short lady with a shiny brown bob and freckled face.

"Hi, everyone!" she said brightly. "My name is Keelie and I'll be leading the tour today. I run the local Chesil Bay Museum and we are over the moon to have so many eager visitors here to see the shipwreck today. It's a small vessel but *highly* significant historically." The History Club shared excited glances. "The museum has been running boat tours of the coastline for over ten years, with the shipwreck being a new addition to the tour. Now I'd just like to run through a quick safety announcement..."

"I think I might sit this trip out..." Zaiba heard her dad mutter to Jessica. "I'll meet you back at the harbour afterwards." His face had turned very pale and he quickly walked off towards solid ground.

Zaiba squeezed Poppy's hand. "I'll be back in one sec," she whispered. "Fill me in on the rest of the instructions."

"Wait!" Zaiba hurried after her dad. "Are you OK?"

Hassan stopped in his tracks and turned round, his face grim. "You know I don't really like boats. I wanted to give it a go, but I think I'm better off waiting here."

Zaiba took her dad's hand. "I've never asked why you're afraid of boats. As a detective, it's my duty to find out."

Hassan chuckled a little, but his eyes were sad. "It's to do with your ammi. But perhaps now isn't the best time."

"No, please, Dad. I'm old enough to know a bit more about when she went ... missing. We've got time before the boat leaves."

Hassan thought for a while and finally took a deep breath. "She was on a mission with the Snow Leopard Detective Agency."

Zaiba nodded and listened intently.

"She had to go into the Sundarbans ... they're these swampy jungles in Bangladesh. The last anyone saw, she took a boat into one of the rivers with a guide. She could swim but those waters are known to be deadly... She was looking for a man who was threatening to destroy the habitat there. He was demolishing the forest and building houses."

Hassan went quiet. Zaiba thought of her ammi. She was definitely the bravest person she'd known.

It made Zaiba want to be even more courageous herself. She gave her dad a big hug and he squeezed her back.

"Thank you for telling me, Dad."

A commotion from a little way up the harbour caught both their attention and they turned to see another boat coming in to dock. It was an off-white colour and slightly larger than the glass-bottom boat. Attached to it was a small blue rowboat, complete with an orange life ring. As soon as the boat had been tied up, three people emerged from the bottom deck, rushing to get off.

"Looks like they're coming this way," Hassan remarked as a woman with the curliest, brightest red hair Zaiba had ever seen bustled towards them.

"Excuse me!" said the woman as she got closer, her skirt billowing round her long legs as she rushed along.

"We're late for the boat tour!" exclaimed a teenager with curly red hair, wearing an anorak and boat shoes.

"The boat's still here so I don't see why we have to run," another teenager groaned. They also had curly red hair but it was cut very short. .

Hassan and Zaiba watched all three of them bundle

on to the boat.

"Here's my brilliant detective observation," Hassan said. "I reckon they're a family. I've never seen two kids who are such a spitting image of their mother!"

"The tour isn't even leaving yet. Why are they in a hurry?" Zaiba shook her head. Rushing often led to mistakes being made – all good detectives knew that.

"Well, I'm glad *I'm* not too late," came a croaky voice, approaching from the harbour passageway.

A tall, thin, elderly gentleman, dressed in a completely unsuitable pinstriped suit and carrying a briefcase, shuffled up to the walkway that led on to the boat. He examined the first step, lifted a foot ... and completely missed the step! He would have toppled over if Zaiba hadn't jumped forward and caught his arm.

"Watch your step, sir," she said politely. "I'll show you the way."

"Oh, thank you!" the man laughed, snorting as he did so. "It's been a while since I've been on a boat!"

Zaiba turned and waved goodbye to her dad before leading the gentleman up on to the deck. When she turned to look at his face she realized he looked familiar. "Have we met before?" Zaiba said.

"No, I don't think so," the man quickly responded. "Uh, you may leave now."

Zaiba's back stiffened at the man's abrupt change of personality. *That was rude!* Then she suddenly caught her breath. She remembered – he was the man she'd seen on the train with the magnifying glass in his briefcase!

"Zaiba, over here!" Poppy called, standing at the very front of the deck looking out to sea. Ali was at her side, checking out a piece of electrical equipment on the floor of the deck. Mariam was sitting next to him cross-legged, already eating her snacks.

Zaiba joined her best friend.

"You didn't miss much in the safety talk. Apart from the fact that the life jackets definitely don't go with my outfit," Poppy pouted.

Ali and Mariam were wearing shorts and sandals but had a light jacket for the wind on the boat. Zaiba had opted for a tunic top Hassan had brought back from his last trip to Pakistan with cut-off leggings. But Poppy wasn't going to miss the chance to dress for a boat trip! She was wearing a striped sky-blue and white sailor dress. She was the best-dressed on board!

"Check out this screen," Ali mused. He was staring at a digital display on the deck. "It's got a temperature reading of the water *and* a speedometer."

"That'll be useful," Mariam said, through munches of an apple. "Because we're about to leave!"

There was a low groaning noise as the boat pulled away from the dock. They were off! Zaiba leaned over the metal railings on the deck as the boat chugged into the small harbour. It was a nice, sunny day but the wind whipped up and she was glad she'd brought her anorak.

Zaiba looked out over the swirling sea. This was her first time on a boat – being out on the water was amazing! She felt like an explorer, looking for new lands on the horizon. The sea was definitely mysterious – who knew what lay hidden in the waters below them? It made Zaiba even more keen to discover what the artefact was before anyone else. In the middle of the deck was a large, glass panel that allowed them to look at the seabed.

Zaiba could only spot seaweed, rocks and sand – for now.

She took out her detective's notebook from her rucksack and flipped it open. She started writing down her initial thoughts.

ARTEFACT?
- Must be an object that can be transported by a small boat. Nothing heavy or bulky!
- Must be made out of material that can last underwater. Could be metal, stone, wood, glass, etc.
- Boat came from Assam, so will be an object made in that place.

"Try some water?" Zaiba heard Jessica behind her. She shut her notebook and turned round to see her stepmum tending to Ali, who had his head over a bucket.

"Water *is* the problem, Mum!" Ali groaned, holding on to his stomach. Zaiba felt sorry for her little brother. He was *not* enjoying the boat trip.

"Seasickness." The woman with bright red curly hair chuckled. "It can sneak up on you if you aren't used to travelling on boats. Sophie used to really suffer from it."

"We live on an island a short distance from here by sea, so now we're used to travelling by boat," Sophie explained.

"Get him to try eating a dry cracker and ask him to look at the horizon," the other red-haired teenager added.

Zaiba smiled. "Thanks for your help."

Just then, Keelie's voice came over the speakers on the boat deck. "OK, everyone! We're approaching the site of the shipwreck. We'll stay over the area for ten minutes, before heading back to shore. So, please make sure you enjoy the view through our glass-bottom viewing panel!"

Zaiba and Poppy rushed over to the panel and peered down into the water. It was murky for sure and there was a lot of seaweed but...

"There! I see the frame!" Zaiba called. Embedded in the sand was the wooden skeleton of an old ship, peeking out at them through the glass. Zaiba's heart raced. If it wasn't for the long mast pole and the familiar shape of the bow, she might not have recognized it as a boat at all.

The excitement of the shipwreck was enough to bring over even the sickest of the passengers, who all stared down into the sea with wonder.

"My goodness!" Ms Talbot exclaimed, overcome with excitement. "It's history right beneath our feet!" She took out her phone and started videoing, narrating as she did so. "Here we are at the site of the historic and ground-breaking underwater excavation," she began, as if she was doing the voiceover on a documentary.

Ali had mustered the strength to crawl over and look down at the wreck. He took his camera from his bag and took a few photos. *Good*, Zaiba thought. *Photographic evidence always comes in handy.*

Zaiba took out her detective's notebook again and began making notes on what she saw. Scraps of ancient yellow material floated and swayed with the current... That had to be the remains of the sails. There were some wooden structures that didn't look like part of the boat's main body. Chests, perhaps? Zaiba wished she could get down into the water for a better look. She'd have to add *scuba diving* to her list of detective skills to learn!

"This area of the coast has long been associated with sailing. Although it's a small port, it has favourable winds and a famous lighthouse on the clifftop," Keelie said over the speaker. "But due to the large amounts of cliff faces and rocky outcrops, the area also attracted less favourable sailors... Smugglers!"

Zaiba and Poppy immediately turned to face each other, their eyes sparkling.

"Smugglers?" Poppy breathed.

"Criminals of the coast!" Zaiba said, her heart beating even faster.

Keelie kept talking. "Smugglers used the rocky cliff face to dock their boats under the cover of night. Many tunnels have been found leading from the cliff up to the town where the smugglers would take the goods for trading. The shipwreck below us was a boat coming in to make a deal with the local smugglers here and has been tracked as an Indian vessel. By carbon dating some samples of wood, we estimate that this ship sunk around 1830. The name *Naseem* means—"

"Breeze," Zaiba said to herself, under her breath.

"Breeze, in Urdu," Keelie echoed on the speakers. Poppy looked at Zaiba and raised her eyebrows, impressed.

As the boat floated over the aged timber of the shipwreck, Zaiba examined it again for any clues.

"Look how rotted the wood is — it's so old!" she heard Katy, one of the History Club members, say.

"I'm searching for any shiny gold coins on the seabed," replied Ivy, another member.

But Zaiba knew they were focusing on the wrong things. She recalled Eden Lockett, in the chapter she'd read last night, studying the old treasure map she'd found. Everyone was focused on the landmarks and searching those for the treasure. But Eden thought differently. "Look at the gaps in between," she had said. "That's where you'll find something that tells a story."

Zaiba followed Eden's advice. She looked at the gaps in between the pieces of wood, the old strips of sail and the bunches of seaweed. Her gaze settled on a gap in between some planks, where she could just make out a black wooden chest, lodged at an angle in the seabed.

There was something marked on the chest in bronze metal ... a symbol that Zaiba recognized.

"E... I... Co..." Zaiba whispered, before her eyes lit up. "*Psst*, Poppy. I know what that symbol is. It's the East India Trading Company."

Poppy squinted at the markings. "Are you sure?"

"Positive." Zaiba kept her voice low. "I've seen it in my history project research loads of times. This boat must have stolen goods from them and brought them here to sell. Let's keep this between us, though. The artefact has been kept a mystery for its own protection. Any information about it could put the museum in peril."

Poppy nodded seriously and mimed zipping her mouth shut.

Zaiba noted down her findings before something else caught her eye. A number of brown hessian sacks lay half covered in sand on the seabed. They might not have looked too interesting but they gave Zaiba an important clue as to what the artefact could be. She also spotted a rusted, half-broken weighing scale poking out from beneath the sacks. Zaiba was on to something!

She added these important clues to the artefact page in her notebook.

ARTEFACT?
- Something traded by the East India Company.
- Brown hessian sacks used to transport loose goods: tea, coffee, sugar, fruit and veg etc.
- Weighing scale: would have been used to cost up price of those goods such as tea, coffee or sugar.

Once the boat started to move again, the breeze dropped and the sun was blazing down on them. It had turned into a very hot day indeed and Ms Talbot was going around all the members of the History Club in turn, making sure they were wearing enough sun cream and drinking lots of water.

"I can't have any of them catching sunstroke on my watch!" she said to Jessica as she went by, bottle of sun cream in hand.

Poppy pulled Zaiba aside and pointed to the family of curly red-haired tourists. They were standing around Keelie at the back of the boat, chatting animatedly about something. Keelie was boxed in by them, her back against the railings of the boat, and though she was smiling Zaiba noticed her eyes darting to the glass-bottom panel of the deck. She obviously wanted to get back to the other visitors.

"Do you think I'd suit red hair?" Poppy asked Zaiba, looking at the family.

"I think your hair looks great as it is," Zaiba chuckled, admiring Poppy's long blond ponytail. "But I do want to know what they're chatting about. Come on!"

Zaiba and Poppy crept closer to the group then leaned on the railings, pretending to look at the sea below.

"And to think the smugglers were on their way to this very coast when the boat sank," the mum was saying. "Whereabouts would they have landed?"

"We aren't sure exactly," Keelie answered. "But we are aware of a few smugglers' tunnels in the cliff face—"

"Oh really?" The woman's face lit up. "I'd love to see them. I'm a bit of a history buff myself."

"Unfortunately, they aren't really open to the public." Keelie smiled. "Even I've not been in one. Maybe in the future. Do you live far?"

"Not really. About twenty minutes away, on Blacksea Island. My name is Jacqueline, by the way. Jacqueline Richards. This is my daughter, Sophie, and my other baby, Leo."

"I'm fourteen, Mum, hardly a baby," Leo replied, rolling their eyes.

"Blacksea Island, did you say? I don't think I've heard of it. Anyway, it's just ... er ... brilliant to have so many fellow historians on board," Keelie replied unsurely, then excused herself and hurried past Jacqueline to the captain's cabin in the middle of the top deck.

Zaiba turned to watch Keelie go and was surprised to see the elderly gentleman she had helped earlier standing close by. He was staring at the coastline with a small pair of ancient-looking binoculars. Another piece of useful equipment stored in that briefcase of his!

Now that she thought about it, Zaiba hadn't seen him come to look at the glass viewing panel once.

"Pops, did you see that man look at the shipwreck?" Zaiba said under her breath, gesturing subtly at the elderly man.

"Hmmm, nope. He just stayed in his seat the whole time, watching everyone." Poppy shrugged. "What's the point of coming on a glass-bottom boat tour if you're just going to watch the passengers and the coastline the whole time?"

Zaiba mulled it over in her head. Her detective instincts were buzzing.

"Maybe he's a people-watcher," Poppy suggested but Zaiba shook her head. Something was odd about the man. Not to mention how quickly he had dismissed Zaiba when she had questioned him. She'd have to keep an eye on him!

Very faintly, muffled behind a half-closed door, Zaiba suddenly became aware of Keelie's voice in the captain's cabin. She must have been chatting to the man driving the boat.

"I might be overthinking it but since we got that note I've been a bit on edge."

Zaiba's ears pricked up and she motioned for Poppy to join her next to the crack in the cabin door. They huddled down behind a large box containing life jackets so they wouldn't be seen listening.

"I mean, what if the person who wrote it is on this boat right now? It gives me the shivers just thinking about it." Keelie sounded worried and though Zaiba couldn't hear the whole conversation, she knew something scary had happened to Keelie – and it involved a menacing note!

"... I know, I know. But the artefact is safe." Keelie sighed and seemed to be regaining her composure.

Zaiba looked at Poppy, her eyes wide. "The museum received a threatening note," she whispered, her heart racing.

"And it's about the artefact," Poppy whispered back.

This was exactly what Zaiba had worried about when they learned of the priceless object! But it was important not to get ahead of themselves. A threatening note was certainly worrying, but it didn't necessarily mean a crime would occur.

"Zaiba, Poppy! We're pulling into the harbour and Ms Talbot wants us all together!" called Ali from the front of the deck, finally revived from his seasickness.

"We'll have to share this with Ali and Mariam. We need to stay on top of any potential threats," Zaiba said, kicking into full detective mode. "But we have to be stealthy. Keelie obviously doesn't want this news to be public."

Poppy nodded in agreement and both girls rushed over to where Ali and Mariam were sitting on the deck.

"Did you know the word nausea comes from the Greek word *naus*, which means ship?" Ali said as soon as Zaiba got close enough to hear him.

Zaiba smiled. "I didn't know. That's actually pretty interesting, but there's something important I need to fill you in on."

Ali and Mariam shared a concerned glance. They knew when Zaiba meant business. They huddled in close, and Zaiba was thankful that the sea breeze would muffle their words from anyone nearby.

"We've overheard news of a threatening note sent to

Keelie about the artefact," Zaiba said in hushed tones.

"A note? What did it say?" Mariam exclaimed.

"Shh!" Poppy warned her. "Keelie seemed to be keeping it hidden — we're not supposed to know about it."

"We don't know much at the moment so we have to keep our eyes and ears open for anything suspicious." Zaiba looked to each of her team in turn.

"What about your mission to discover what the artefact actually is?" Ali asked her.

Zaiba thought for a moment. "It's still on. If we want to protect the artefact from a potential threat, it would help to know what it is first!"

She rummaged in her backpack and pulled out her notebook. "Here's the plan."

<u>Phase One</u> – Identify mystery artefact.
<u>Phase Two</u> – The note! What did it say? Who sent it and why?
<u>Phase Three</u> – Protect the artefact until it's shipped to Assam.

They stared at the notebook, taking in each stage and nodding in agreement.

"I'm in," Mariam said seriously.

"So am I," Ali added quickly.

Zaiba looked at Poppy who laughed. "You already know I'm in!"

Zaiba smiled at her team and put the notebook away safely in her pocket. "Then let's do this!"

The boat was pulling into the harbour now. Zaiba, Poppy, Ali and Mariam joined the rest of their class, heads still buzzing with the latest development.

"I hope you were all looking out for clues about the mystery artefact," Ms Talbot announced to her assembled group. "I know I have some promising leads."

A few heads nodded but Zaiba was pretty sure that only she had spotted the crucial clue on the chest. Everyone else seemed to be excitedly murmuring about gold coins. Besides, there might be an even bigger mystery at hand now!

"And I hope you haven't had enough of the sea yet," Ms Talbot continued, "because I thought we could go for a swim!"

The group cheered, even the ones who had spent most of the trip feeling seasick.

Zaiba joined in, though she stole a look back at the Richards as they disembarked the boat, carrying a picnic basket.

She looked round for the older gentleman too, but he'd already melted away into the crowd of tourists. *Odd*, Zaiba thought. *Who knew he could move so fast?*

4
THE VOICE INSIDE THE CLIFF

As soon as they'd arrived at the beach, Hassan had produced a brand-new cricket bat and ball from a large shopping bag and started a game of beach cricket.

"Ali, on your left!" Hassan called, pointing towards the sky.

Ali sped barefoot in the sand. As fast as he could he headed after the ball that thundered towards him. Everyone held their breath...

"Got it!" he cried, catching the ball with one hand.

Zaiba dropped her bat. She'd been caught out!

Ms Talbot had nominated herself to be the referee and had set up a beach chair overlooking the match. Now she called out words of encouragement. "I say, well played, old chap!" she cried to Ali, who bowed in response.

"I'm just going to hand out the snacks," Jessica called, sitting on another beach chair well out of the way of any flying cricket balls.

"I think I need a snack break! Someone fill in for me," Ali called, running over to Jessica. Since Zaiba was already out she went over as well. Anil, their B&B host, had made samosas and cucumber sandwiches — 'a real blend of East and West' as Hassan had said.

"I really want to explore the rocks at the base of the cliff. I could find a fossil!" Ali said through bites of a sandwich. "Can I go, Mum?"

Jessica thought about it for a moment. "Only if Zaiba goes with you."

"No problem," Zaiba said quickly, slipping on her flip-flops. She couldn't wait to get over to the cliffs! This was the perfect opportunity to see if she could find any of the smugglers' secret tunnels that Keelie had mentioned on the boat tour. It was the logical next step in Phase

One of the mission – the tunnels could provide clues to the mystery artefact. If they were cavernous, the object might be something very large. But a narrow, winding tunnel would mean the object had to be small enough to be smuggled through. She wouldn't know unless she got a good look!

Ali and Zaiba headed over to the base of the cliff, a short walk away from the group and still close enough that Jessica could keep an eye on them.

"What are you up to?" Poppy said, running to join Zaiba, trying to catch her breath. Mariam was close behind her.

"I thought you were still playing cricket?" Zaiba replied, shielding her eyes from the sun.

Mariam pouted. "Our team dropped out. They got distracted by the snacks!"

"Anyway, a cricket match is boring when there's detective work going on!" Poppy winked.

"I'm searching for fossils!" Ali said, bending over to examine the ground.

"And I'm trying to see if I can find the entrance to one

of the smugglers' tunnels," Zaiba explained. "I'd like to look inside."

"Then let's go rock climbing!" Mariam announced.

Off they went, picking their way across the hard rocks and slimy seaweed with Ali keeping an eye out for fossils. Zaiba kept her focus on the cliff face, looking out for any cracks or openings that might mark the entrance to a tunnel. Occasionally, she would turn round and wave at Jessica, just to make sure she knew they were all right. A little way along, Zaiba noticed a white etching.

"Look, it's a fish." Zaiba ran her hand over the etching that looked as though it had been engraved in the cliff with a sharp implement. "It sort of looks like an arrow, with the fish head pointing that way..."

"Graffiti!" Mariam said, looking at the etching disapprovingly.

"Ancient graffiti," Poppy corrected her. "Maybe it's Roman?"

Zaiba shook her head. "Keelie was saying on the boat tour that the smugglers used carvings as a code to show the tubsman, the guy who actually hauled the goods ashore, where the tunnels were. Hmmm." She felt her mind whirring. "If they needed multiple people to handle the goods, the mystery artefact might have been something heavy..."

Ali looked at Poppy and Zaiba dubiously. "Or it could just have been some kids with a sharp stone?"

Poppy looked disappointed. "That's less exciting."

Still, the gang picked their way along the cliff face in the direction indicated by the fish etching. Not far ahead Zaiba could see a crack in the cliff. The sea ran into the crack, the opening surrounded by sharp rocks jutting out of the surf. It could be the entrance of a tunnel! But Zaiba would have to swim over if she wanted to find out, and that definitely wouldn't be safe. Especially as they were now out of sight of Jessica and the rest of the group. Zaiba knew that her stepmum would be wondering where they were.

She was just about to suggest they turn back when a muffled sound caught her attention. She froze. "What's that? Can you hear it?" Her heart was suddenly hammering in her chest.

All four of them stood still as statues, listening hard. It sounded like a voice yelling.

"Where's it coming from?" Zaiba whirled round and scanned the beach. But she couldn't see anyone shouting.

The shouts were clearer now. They followed a pattern: "Hai ya! Hai! Hai! HAAAIIIII YAAAAA!"

It sounded to Zaiba like they were echoing from *inside* the cliff.

"Whoever it is, they sound *angry*." Ali shuddered.

"No, they sound *threatening*," Poppy said pointedly. Zaiba knew what her best friend was hinting at.

"You think the shouting and the threatening note are connected? It's definitely suspicious." Zaiba put her ear to the cliff. "I think they're inside here... Maybe in a cave? If only we could get in!" It was so frustrating!

"Whoa! Watch out!"

Another yell – this time it definitely came from the beach.

"We should get back," she said. They couldn't get into the cave and people would be worrying about them. Besides, the shouting had stopped now.

She led the group back the way they'd come and saw Hassan talking to a group of people sitting on the ground. A group of people with curly red hair.

Zaiba, Poppy, Ali and Mariam ran back along the beach to the group, slowing when they got to where the Richards were having a picnic. As they got closer, it became clear what had happened – Hassan's cricket game had got him in trouble with the Richards. They had a big cream trifle on their picnic blanket and splat in the middle of it was his cricket ball!

The rest of the History Club had stayed back by their towels with Ms Talbot but were watching as Hassan tried to retrieve the ball. They'd sent him to do the apologizing!

"Once again, I really am so sorry," Hassan said as he reached down to extract the ball from the cream.

Jacqueline Richards waved her hand dismissively. "Oh, no problem at all! We're all just having fun on the beach." But Zaiba noticed a vein popping on the woman's forehead from where she was forcing a smile.

Hassan looked relieved to see Zaiba approaching.

"Ah, kids – there you are. Did you see anything interesting by the rocks?"

"We heard a—" Ali began but Poppy nudged him to be quiet.

"We were looking for the entrance to the smugglers' tunnels but the closest we got was finding some carvings in the rocks," Zaiba stepped in.

Jacqueline laughed. "Smugglers' tunnels! You know, I think Keelie is making it all up. Probably helps them draw more tourists to the museum."

"Really?" Zaiba was confused – the teenagers' mum had sounded so excited to visit them.

"Trust me, I would know if there really were tunnels. I've been to many different historical sites just like this one and tunnels are rare," Jacqueline explained. "We're historians and collectors, you see. Our house is virtually a museum!"

"What she means, is everything in our house is basically falling apart," Sophie said, laughing.

"Very fun to bring your mates around to…" Leo mumbled.

Zaiba smiled, although she felt a little sorry for Leo who clearly wasn't as keen on history as Sophie and Jacqueline were.

"Well, we'll see you around then." Hassan waved, but once they were out of earshot he added, "That lady is scarily intense."

Zaiba agreed. Jacqueline seemed certain that the tunnels weren't real but Zaiba wasn't so sure. How else would the smugglers on the *Naseem* have planned to transport their goods inland without being seen? And that carving looked as if it could be important... She definitely had a lot to think about.

They rejoined the group and everyone changed back into their normal clothes. Ali wrapped himself in his beach towel and was wriggling around on the ground, trying to slip off his swimming trunks.

"Ali, just put your trousers on top of the trunks," Hassan laughed. "You look like a worm!"

"Don't worry, Dad – I'm nearly..." A damp pair of trunks suddenly appeared out of his towel and he held them up, proudly. "There! Ta-dah!" He looked like a magician who'd pulled a bunch of flowers out of thin air! Everyone started laughing and pretty soon, the whole History Club were wrapped in their towels, doing exactly the same thing as Ali.

Zaiba and Poppy could barely get changed themselves, they were too busy giggling at the sight of everyone wriggling around!

Once Zaiba had finally managed to get her normal clothes on, she let her mind wander back to the shouts they had heard in the cliffs. The sound of it echoed around inside her head. She gazed across the beach, back towards the rocks. The cliff face loomed up into the sky, casting a dark shadow over the sea and looking almost a little creepy. She was too far away to see the crack but she knew it was there – and so did someone else. Someone who was in a concealed cave. The shouts, the mystery artefact and Keelie receiving a threatening note – all three of these details felt connected. The certainty of it tingled in her detective bones.

Who had been in the cliff?

And what had they been shouting about?

5
SMUGGLERS' SECRETS

It had been a long day already but there was no rest
for the History Club or budding detectives! There was
a mystery artefact to uncover and Phase One wouldn't
complete itself. The History Club, still sandy and a bit
soggy from the beach, trooped up to the museum on the
clifftop.

As they approached their destination, Zaiba was
amazed. It was as though they'd stepped back in time!

"I thought this was a museum," Poppy said, gazing up
at the two old structures in front of them.

"I think it *is*," Zaiba replied, eyeing up the posters
on the walls and the sign over a doorway that said

'Entrance'. She clicked on her voice recorder and made a note: "Observations. We are now at Chesil Bay Museum. There's one main point of entry – the front gate. We are standing in the courtyard. One larger building on the right of the courtyard is L-shaped. There is another smaller building on the left-hand side. In between the buildings, and straight ahead, I can see a small road, some parked cars and the cliff edge. The buildings look old. *Really old*. They're made of white stone and black beams. There are no clues as to where the mystery artefact is being held." Zaiba clicked off the recorder.

"This is a living museum," Ms Talbot explained, coming to stand before the group. "The buildings are the original structures from the eighteenth century and all the staff who work here dress up like people from that time period. You'll learn more about this tomorrow in our tour before we see the unveiling of the mystery artefact."

"So, we will have a chance to properly explore the museum before the reveal?" Zaiba asked. She was keen to make sure she could do a thorough investigation of the place the artefact was being kept. Mostly to make sure it was safely stored away, but also to give her some clues as to what it might be. Ms Talbot had challenged them to guess what the artefact was before the unveiling, so the tour around the museum would be her absolute last chance at identifying it correctly.

Beneath her sun hat, Ms Talbot's eyes glittered. "We're here for something exciting. Everyone attending the grand reveal tomorrow has been invited to a special play that's being put on this evening. What do you think of that?"

The whole group cheered, the sound echoing around the museum's courtyard, where people in old-style dresses and uniforms hurried about. Zaiba caught Poppy gazing in wonder at the clothes. She had a feeling that her friend's next History Club project was going to involve making an eighteenth-century outfit!

But something else had caught Zaiba's eye. A black van was parked on the small road that ran along the outside of both buildings. The logo on the back read 'Sikora Security Solutions'.

"Look, the museum has hired extra security," Zaiba whispered to Poppy. "Do you think it's to protect the priceless artefact?"

"Or extra muscle brought in after Keelie got the note?" Poppy whispered back, raising her eyebrows.

But there was no time to ponder. Ms Talbot clapped her hands together to get everyone's attention back to her. "Now, my fellow historians," she sang. "The play is called *Smugglers' Secrets* and is a dramatic re-enactment of the sinking of the *Naseem*! The play will show us how the smugglers obtained the artefact and transported it to these waters. Of course, the story will not reveal the identity of the object, but I'm sure we'll get some important clues as to what it could be!"

"It's just like in Eden Lockett's *The Cottage on the Cliff*!" Zaiba gasped, squeezing Poppy's hand.

"When Eden goes undercover in the local theatre group's play to gather inside knowledge!" Poppy squeezed Zaiba's hand back and even jumped up and down enthusiastically.

Zaiba beamed. This was the *perfect* opportunity to identify the mystery artefact! She'd probably be able to work it out even before the museum tour tomorrow.

Ali raised a hand. "Is that lady part of the living museum?" He pointed towards a woman who was standing across the courtyard from them on a little box, shouting. Zaiba hadn't noticed her before – she had been too busy watching the museum staff in their costumes. But now she looked closer, Zaiba could see that this woman was different. She held a placard that definitely didn't look as though it was from the eighteenth century. Not with those bright poster paints! The sign read in very messy handwriting:

> Artefact stays here!
> Don't give away
> our history!

"I'm surprised anyone could read the sign with that handwriting!" Ms Talbot did not seem impressed at all.

Zaiba listened in to what the woman was saying. Everyone in the courtyard seemed to be doing their best to ignore her, but Zaiba wanted to know why she seemed angry.

"The artefact was found in OUR waters!" the woman called out. "It's already brought tourists to the area, think of how it would boost our economy to keep it here. They want to send it across the world but OUR divers found it!"

She seemed very keen on pointing out what belonged to who. Her voice sounded hoarse from shouting.

"But why would they keep the artefact here when it came from India?" Zaiba puzzled aloud. "It doesn't make sense. It must be something really rare for her to want to keep it here."

"Did you know that many of the artefacts in the UK's biggest museums were taken without permission?" Ali said.

"Taken without permission... Isn't that another word for 'stolen'?" Zaiba said, a little shocked. She'd devoted her life to seeing justice done! It seemed wrong that some museums didn't feel the same way. "What do you think, Jessica?"

Zaiba's stepmum was an artist and there was pretty much nothing she didn't know about museums and galleries.

Jessica shared a glance with Hassan. "It can be ... very complicated," she said, placing her hands on Zaiba's shoulders. She gave a gentle squeeze. "Some of those items were taken a long time ago and so the people who run the museums now don't think they should be punished for mistakes made in the past. It takes a lot of discussion between countries and willingness to work together."

Zaiba thought back to what she'd learned about the East India Trading Company. Lots of the treasures and important artefacts they stole from India all those years ago were still in houses and museums across the UK today. Maybe the people who owned them now didn't feel guilty because they'd had them for such a long time. But in Zaiba's opinion as a detective, even crimes that happened a long time ago should be accounted for. It was a lot to think about...

One of the actors, dressed in a brown tabard and leggings, emerged from a low doorway, ringing a handbell. "Five minutes until the show starts!" he called.

Zaiba was longing to ask her stepmum more about museums, but she had to keep her mind focused and alert for any clues in the play!

Their group was led across the museum's courtyard and through the gap between the buildings. They walked right up to the cliff edge, where there were steps cut into the rock.

Zaiba walked down the steps and was surprised when a big, open-air theatre appeared in front of her. It was carved into the clifftop and overlooked the sea! Zaiba realized they must be standing right above where they'd been exploring on the beach earlier.

"Wow!" Zaiba and Poppy breathed in unison.

The actors in the play were also working as ushers, showing everyone to their seats on wooden benches, arranged in rows leading down to the stage. The man in the brown tabard led Zaiba, Poppy, Ali, Mariam, Hassan and Jessica to a row near the bottom of the steps.

"Are you in the play?" Zaiba enquired. She noticed he was still wearing his staff badge that showed his name, Connor.

"Yes, I am," Connor replied in a surprisingly deep voice. "I am in every production the museum puts on. I'm sort of known as *the* actor in town." Connor brushed a lock of hair back from his face importantly and Zaiba guessed he was putting on the deep voice to seem more impressive.

"You must know a lot about local history then," Zaiba said, seeing if she could get any information out of their new acquaintance.

"Oh yes, absolutely. In fact, I make sure each play is one hundred per cent accurate to the time period. With the recent influx of tourists we've had a much bigger audience, so it's especially important to be absolutely correct." Zaiba noticed that Connor's eyes gleamed when he said the word 'audience'. This guy clearly loved the spotlight.

"So, you're playing a smuggler..." Poppy chimed in. "I can tell because your costume is in dark colours so you aren't as noticeable, and you have a hessian sack tied to your belt."

Zaiba was seriously impressed with Poppy's historical fashion knowledge!

"The only difference is your shoes have plastic soles," Poppy continued. "But a smuggler's shoes would have been leather."

Connor's expression darkened. "My costume is completely authentic! So what if my shoes have plastic soles?"

Zaiba and Poppy looked at Connor in silence, taken aback by his outburst. In the moment, he'd forgotten to put on his deep, serious actor voice, and now it sounded high and rasping.

Connor suddenly turned red. "Now, if you'll excuse me, I have vocal exercises to do."

As Zaiba and Poppy took their seats, they looked at each other in amazement.

"Wow, Connor definitely puts the *drama* in *dramatic*,"

Poppy commented.

"Either that or he doesn't like being questioned." Zaiba narrowed her eyes and watched the actor warming up with the rest of the cast down on the stage.

Ali had positioned himself between their mum and dad, so there were six of them sharing the bench. The rest of the History Club sat in front of them, with Ms Talbot doing her best to keep them from chattering too much. There was another group of adults, all wearing T-shirts that said 'Tolworth Time Team!'. They seemed the most excited out of everyone, loudly discussing the history of the museum and sitting near the front of the stage. Zaiba guessed they were a history club too – only they were all adults and very serious about it.

"I asked for sweet *and* salty popcorn. This is just sweet!" a woman complained loudly behind Zaiba.

She turned around and saw Jacqueline, sitting at the back of the auditorium and holding out a box of popcorn to a very nervous-looking teen selling snacks. *The Richards did they say were history fans. They must be coming to the grand reveal too,* Zaiba thought.

"Sorry, madam, I'll change that for you right away," the teen responded and hurried off.

Jacqueline noticed that heads had turned to look her way and blushed a little. Her children went bright red and sunk down in their seats. Zaiba once again noticed how similar they all looked. From far away it was hard to tell them apart.

The sun had lowered in the sky and an announcement came over the speakers. "Esteemed guests, today's performance of *Smugglers' Secrets* is about to begin! Please switch off your phones, relax and take a trip back in history to 1715..."

"The Lander's in place, mind the sails!"

"Heave ho! Put yer back into it, lads!"

"We'll meet One-Eyed Jack at the Chesil Inne. He'll be waitin'."

"I'll give ye no more than the asking price for the lot. It could be the finest tea in the world fer all I care!"

"The wind is too high, we're for it! Man overboard!"

Zaiba was in theatre heaven! A play all about mystery, secret tunnels and stopping crime – this was her perfect evening. The play included a musical number, where all the people at the inn sang a sea shanty and did a dance. There was even a dog actor at one point! The scene when the ship overturned and sunk into the waves (which were recreated with billowing silk scarves) was particularly thrilling and a tiny bit scary.

When the play finally ended, Zaiba felt as though she'd been on a journey through time. The audience gave the actors a huge round of applause, with Connor as One-Eyed Jack taking a second deep bow and blowing kisses to the audience. Zaiba thought he was overdoing it a bit.

Best of all, the play had helped Zaiba with her mission! There had been an inn scene where the smugglers were trading hessian sacks full of tea. This had given Zaiba the final clue she needed about the mystery artefact. She was now certain the weighing scales and sacks she'd seen on the shipwreck meant the *Naseem* had been carrying tea stolen from the East India Company. And what priceless artefact could be linked to tea? She could have hugged herself! *This might be a record time for solving a mystery*, she thought. She was desperate to announce her guess to the History Club before they went to the big reveal the next day. Being able to explain how she'd worked it out using her detective instincts would be so much fun! Zaiba didn't like to admit it but she also wanted to show off just a *tiny bit* to her friends and teacher.

As they left the theatre and were queuing on the stairs with the other audience members, Zaiba suddenly became aware of someone she hadn't noticed before. The elderly gentleman was queuing up ahead, briefcase in hand and surveying his surroundings. "That's strange," Zaiba thought aloud. "I don't remember seeing him earlier when the play started."

Poppy followed her eyeline and squinted at the elderly gentleman. "Oh, I saw him. Or did I? It could have been a different man..."

The queue started to move again and Zaiba put it out of her mind. While they were waiting for the bus to take them back to the B&B, she made a deal with herself. *I'll reveal the identity of the mystery artefact tonight at dinner!*

She couldn't help smiling to herself.

"What are you grinning at?" Ali said.

"Oh, nothing!" Zaiba said in an innocent, sing-song voice.

Her little brother's eyes narrowed. "You're up to something, I can tell. You always look like that when you're detecting."

"Like what?" She genuinely didn't know.

"Like you're having more fun than anyone else in the entire world," he said.

Zaiba smiled to herself again. She couldn't help it if detecting made her happy. Aunt Fouzia had called it ... what was it again? A calling. Could Zaiba help it if she was just born to do this? It ran in the blood, straight from her ammi. And this calling meant that Zaiba had been able to work out what the mystery artefact was! She was absolutely sure of it. Getting her notebook out of her rucksack, Zaiba opened it to the page where she'd written their plan and put a tick next to the first line.

"Phase one? Complete."

6
FROM ASSAM TO CHESIL BAY

"Fifteen minutes to get washed and then I want everyone in the dining room!" Ms Talbot left the History Club with strict instructions once they'd got back into the B&B. After a full day out, everyone was definitely ready for dinner!

The anticipation of revealing the identity of the artefact was filling Zaiba with nervous energy and she got changed in a flash. Even if she had correctly figured out phase one of her mission, she had to get phase two under way. What did the note say, and who had sent it? Those questions were now at the top of her list.

"I'm going down early, there's something I want to ask the Duttas about," she said, grabbing a notebook and pen.

"OK, see you there," Poppy replied, holding up different jumper options in front of the mirror.

Ali and Mariam were up on the top bunk, engrossed in a zombie game on Ali's phone, and didn't even look up as Zaiba slipped out of the room.

Down in the dining room, Anil and Khushi were setting out plates and laying the table.

"You're a bit early, Zaiba." Khushi looked surprised to see her standing in the doorway.

"I was wondering if I could ask you about something," Zaiba said. "I can help you set things out?"

This was a technique Zaiba had learned from Eden Lockett. People are more likely to talk when they're focused on an activity.

"Well, of course. What's on your mind?" Anil handed Zaiba a stack of glasses to put on the table.

"There was a woman today at the museum who said that the artefact they found in the shipwreck should stay here. But it came from India... So surely it should be go back there?" Zaiba shook her head slightly, still trying to understand the woman's point of view.

"The people here in Chesil Bay are very proud of their history," Anil said seriously.

"Especially their seafaring history," Khushi added. "But that doesn't change the fact that the artefact belongs where it was originally made."

Zaiba hesitated, unsure of how to phrase her next question. "So, nothing should leave the place it was made ever? It's just that, we have some things from Pakistan at home my dad brought with him and ... I've noticed you have some paintings and ornaments here that look like they are from India too."

Anil and Khushi shared a look before Khushi spoke.

"Those are family pieces, *beti*. We brought those with us, as I'm sure your father did too, to remind us of home and keep our culture close to us." Khushi patted Zaiba's hand.

"I think I understand." Zaiba paused, waiting to ask

the most important question. "You said that the locals here are proud of their history. You don't think anyone would plan to … take the artefact for themselves, do you?"

Anil and Khushi looked concerned. "I don't think so. Why, have you heard something?" Anil cocked his head to one side.

Zaiba opened her mouth to speak, but the sound of thundering footsteps coming down the stairs signalled an end to the conversation – the History Club was ready for dinner!

"No, I didn't hear anything. I was just wondering. Thank you." Zaiba forced a smile and quickly walked off, finding a seat for her and Poppy.

"Did you speak to the Duttas?" Poppy asked, plonking herself down in the chair next to Zaiba's.

"Yeah, what did you ask them about?" Ali said, wriggling on to the other empty chair.

"I'll tell you later – phase two stuff! But now, let's eat!" Zaiba had caught sight of the massive steaming bowl of coconut rice that Anil was carrying out. Khushi was close behind, laden with an assortment of bowls containing fragrant sauces and golden fried delicacies.

Zaiba looked around the room where everyone was gathered. This was the perfect time to share her findings. A detective always needed a full audience!

"Ms Talbot," Zaiba said, politely raising her hand. "Since we'll be going to the unveiling of the artefact tomorrow, I wondered if I could share my theory about what it could be?"

A hush fell over the room and Ms Talbot looked at Zaiba, wide-eyed. "Well, of course. But I can't imagine how you've worked it out without even going into the museum yet! Not even *I* have come to a definite conclusion..."

Zaiba stood up and cleared her throat, glancing down at her notebook once more to jog her memory. Her friends all gazed at her, mouths open, waiting to see what she would say next. Even Ali managed to resist stealing a bit of the coconut rice.

Zaiba began. "On the glass-bottom boat tour, something caught my eye. I noticed a wooden casket with the symbol for the East India Trading Company on it. The boat also had an Urdu name – *Naseem*. Urdu is spoken mainly in India and Pakistan."

Zaiba paused and glanced at Poppy. Her friend gave her two thumbs up. Zaiba smiled and continued.

"So we know the boat is of Indian origin and too small to be an East India Trading Company ship, which were very large vessels. So why was it carrying their goods? Well, since it was headed to a known smugglers' cove, it seems likely to me that the artefact is a stolen item."

"Then I noticed hessian sacks for transportation, along with some measuring scales. This indicated that the goods on board were something that could be measured and poured. When we were watching the play, the smugglers in the inn were trading stolen tea. Keelie said the boat came from Assam and a quick Google search showed me that Assam is one of the world's leading tea growing regions. I also know that the East India Trading Company was the main exporter of tea to the UK in 1830 when the ship sunk—"

Ms Talbot interrupted. "So you think the mystery artefact is tea? But it wouldn't have survived this long in the water."

Zaiba already knew that and she shook her head. "No. I think the mystery artefact is something to *do* with tea..." She glanced around the room. Everyone was watching her. Even Anil and Khushi stood framed in the kitchen doorway, arms folded, listening intently. "A tea*pot*."

The whole of the History Club burst into laughter.

"You really think the priceless artefact is a *teapot?*" said James, one of the members.

"Yes. I've been doing my project on teapots and they have a fascinating history. The earlier models were made of precious materials. If this teapot is *really* valuable it could be made of something like ivory," Zaiba explained.

But everyone was still chuckling. Even Ms Talbot looked sceptical. Zaiba couldn't understand why – she had used her knowledge of history to work it out. But then Zaiba realized – Ms Talbot had desperately wanted to figure it out first herself.

"I believe you, Zaiba," Poppy chimed in, glaring at the rest of the History Club.

"Teapots can be valuable," Ali added. "The world's most expensive teapot is worth three million dollars." He shrugged. "It's in *Guinness World Records*."

Zaiba sat down in her chair, deflated. No one else believed her.

Hassan and Jessica smiled at her encouragingly from across the room but they had to support her – they were her parents.

"Don't worry, Zaiba. They'll see tomorrow at the unveiling," Poppy whispered in her ear. "Just you wait."

Zaiba took a deep breath and nodded. Poppy was right. They just had to wait for the unveiling at the museum. It would be a teapot, definitely... Wouldn't it? For the first time in her career as a detective, Zaiba felt a butterfly tremor of doubt. Could she possibly have got it wrong?

Later that night, before going to bed, she quickly video-called Aunt Fouzia from the bathroom. It wasn't the ideal place to hold a meeting but it was the only way she could be alone. She closed the toilet seat lid and perched there – so undignified for a detective! Still, she felt better when Aunt Fouzia reminded her of the time she'd had to hide in an industrial waste bin behind a famous restaurant in Lahore.

"It was so embarrassing," Aunt Fouzia said. "When the waiters pulled me out, I had a banana skin on my head!" She looked fondly at Zaiba from the screen. "Now tell me, little one. What's making you unhappy?"

Zaiba hadn't even said anything yet! How could her aunt possibly know she was unhappy?

Aunt Fouzia answered her question before she'd even spoken it out loud. "I can always tell, you know," she said, wagging a finger. "You develop the cutest little crease between your eyebrows." She mimed a little crease between her own eyebrows and Zaiba couldn't help giggling.

She told her aunt about her theories and how the whole of the History Club had laughed at her.

"But you'll find out the truth tomorrow, right?"

Aunt Fouzia prompted.

"Right."

"Well, then. Go to bed and enjoy knowing that the truth is still yours alone for a few more hours. It's a very special gift for a detective – to know things before anyone else. What a privilege!" She winked at Zaiba. "I have every faith in you." She ended the call and Zaiba slid from the toilet seat, holding her phone beneath her arm.

She looked in the mirror and reminded herself what a lucky girl she was. She had a loving family, she led the UK branch of a detective agency, and she had a secret to hug to herself all night. Oh, and tomorrow she could enjoy using the four best words in the English language.

I told you so!

7

A DISAPPEARING ACT

The air was fresh with the sea breeze and the sun shining as the History Club arrived at the museum the next morning. They were to be given a full tour of the living museum before they attended the unveiling ceremony with a few other lucky tourists who had managed to get tickets. Ms Talbot had promised they could all have another game of beach cricket after the artefact had been revealed!

They queued up in the courtyard and Ms Talbot handed out lanyards with 'GUEST' written on them.

"I feel like a VIP!" Poppy beamed, hanging the lanyard round her neck. "This is like the time me and

Mum got backstage passes, when we went to see Maysoon in concert! I'm glad we dressed up for the occasion."

Since this was an unveiling *ceremony*, Poppy had convinced Zaiba to wear her fanciest patterned top and cropped leggings. Poppy had opted for a stylish summer jumpsuit. Mariam was wearing her favourite spotty dress and Ali said that it was too hot to wear anything but shorts and a T-shirt, so he'd done just that.

"It *is* nice to be treated like an honoured guest." Zaiba eyed her lanyard approvingly, though she thought it would be more fitting if hers said 'SECURITY'.

"So, what phase of the plan are we on now, Zaiba?" Mariam said quietly, checking over her shoulder to make sure no one was listening.

Zaiba got out her notebook and looked over their plan. "Well, phase one is complete, whether Ms Talbot believes me or not. So, now that we have a pretty good idea what the artefact is—"

"A teapot!" Ali said, beaming. Zaiba couldn't help but smile back at him. She was always grateful for his support.

"Right, a teapot. We can move on to phase two – the threatening note that was sent to Keelie. We need to find out what it said, so we can assess how much of a real threat it is ... and who sent it."

"A tour of the museum is the perfect opportunity for snooping around and finding any potential leads." Poppy rubbed her hands together. "I do love to snoop!"

Zaiba laughed and snapped her notebook shut. She was blessed to have a best friend that loved detecting almost as much as she did!

"Observation time," Zaiba said, opening the voice recorder on her phone. "We are on location at Chesil Bay Museum. In the courtyard, there are lots of actors wandering about in character, sweeping the floor and pretending to sell fruit and vegetables from a cart. The woman protesting yesterday is here again, standing on a box and shouting about the artefact staying in Chesil Bay. Two men are talking to her, both wearing shirts, ties and smart trousers." Zaiba stopped recording so that she could listen to the conversation.

"Come on, ma'am. You've been at this every day..."

the taller of the men was saying.

"You know we can't have you here during the unveiling. The press will be here," the shorter one reasoned.

They must be the security guards the museum has brought in, Zaiba thought. But her observations were cut short by a woman in a brown scruffy dress with puffy underskirts approaching their group.

"Morning, everyone!" Her eyes twinkled. "My name is Marie the Barmaid and I'll be showing you round the inn today," she said in a strong local accent.

Marie the Barmaid took the History Club into the largest building and started telling them all about the history of the place. She stayed in character when she interacted with the other actors, even telling someone sweeping the floors to, "Put some welly in it, boy!" The inside of the inn was laid out with wooden chairs and tables, and barrels that would have stored drink behind the bar.

"It really is like going back in time," Zaiba whispered.

"Yeah... It even smells damp and musty like an old inn." Poppy held her nose.

Marie heard Poppy and assured them that the aroma was as fresh as a new week's cog of ale, a delivery of shrimps and rats' droppings. It smelled a bit like Ali's hamster cage when he hadn't cleaned it out in a week!

Ms Talbot raised her hand, which Zaiba found very funny for a teacher, and asked their guide a question. "What was the inn used for between the 1800s and the present day?"

The tour guide hesitated. After all, if she stayed in character she wouldn't be able to answer the question.

"Well," she muttered. "After the inn partially burned down, it was empty until it was rebuilt. Then it became a fishermen's warehouse for a while – that's why it has all these hooks here for smoking and curing." Marie gestured to the ceiling.

"MARIE!" a voice bellowed from the doorway.

Zaiba whirled round to see Connor – the actor who had snapped at them the day before – glowering at Marie.

"I need to talk to you for a minute, Barmaid. Now!" He was still using his smuggler persona but Zaiba wasn't sure that even smugglers needed to be so rude.

"Excuse me, everyone." Marie had gone bright red. She bobbed in a slight curtsey to the History Club then scurried over to Connor, who began talking to her in hushed but aggressive tones.

The History Club wandered about the room, looking at the various artefacts kept in cabinets. There was an ancient masthead, a fishing net and a row of green glass bottles with glass ball stoppers in them. It was all fascinating, but Zaiba wanted to hear more of the conversation going on between Marie and Connor...

She casually wandered closer to the doorway that the actors had disappeared through and busied herself looking at an old iron mug in one of the display cabinets.

"The instructions are clear, Brenda — *never* break character. And where is your bonnet?" Connor was hissing.

So, Marie's real name was Brenda.

"Sorry, Connor, but they asked a question," Brenda answered in protest. "And my bonnet disappeared from the staff room yesterday."

"Ugh, typical! The modern times part of the tour comes at the *end*. How are they supposed to get an authentic experience if you break character and don't wear the correct costume? We have so many more tourists here at the moment because of the artefact, plus the press! This could be my – I mean, the *museum*'s – chance to be discovered. Don't mess this up!"

Zaiba could hear Connor stomp back out into the courtyard. *Wow.* Connor didn't just take acting seriously, he was hoping to use the mystery artefact to get his big break into stardom! She felt bad for Brenda who was standing in the doorway to the inn, looking frustrated. Before she knew it, Zaiba was walking over to her.

"Hi, are you OK? He seems quite ... intense." Zaiba smiled. "We're really enjoying your tour!"

Brenda stiffened at first but then she let out a huge sigh. "Yes, thank you. I'm sorry you had to hear that."

Zaiba was pleased that Brenda seemed all right, but she was here to do some detecting and she had to find out about that note. Now could be a good time to implement a skill Aunt Fouzia had taught her.

"Everyone must be extra stressed at the moment, with the mystery artefact being stored here and Keelie receiving that note..." Zaiba trailed off, pretending to be casual but keeping one eye on Brenda.

The barmaid gasped. "How do you know about the note?" she whispered.

Zaiba repressed a smile. Aunt Fouzia's technique worked! Dropping a secret and pretending you know more than you do to find out information – genius!

"Oh, rumours are going around ... but what exactly did it say?" Zaiba kept her voice low, aware that Brenda would be in trouble if she was caught talking to her.

"I shouldn't really tell you, but ... it was scrawled in red pen. It said, *You'd better keep the artefact safe. Who knows what could happen?*" Brenda shuddered. "Some people think it was just a practical joke but I'm not sure."

Zaiba made a mental note to write the message down in her notebook. "I'm sure the artefact's fine. Nice talking to you, Bren—I mean, Marie."

Brenda suddenly seemed aware of how much she'd slipped out of character on the job. She straightened her skirt and lifted her chin high, getting back into the role of Marie the Barmaid. Then she raised her voice and called to the group. "Thanks for visiting but I gotta kick you out of the inn now! You're wanted in the Great Hall." She pointed at an adjoining room before scurrying away.

"The unveiling ceremony!" Ms Talbot clapped her hands together. "Time to find out what that artefact is, once and for all." She looked at Zaiba before heading into the other room. Ms Talbot *really* didn't believe it was a teapot, but no one else had any other suggestions.

"Don't worry, darling." Jessica came up behind her.

"Oh, I'm not," Zaiba reassured her. Last night's chat with Aunt Fouzia had helped with that.

As they walked single file into the Great Hall, Zaiba whispered into Poppy's ear, "I found out what the note said. Phase two is nearly complete. But let's focus on phase three now, since it's the most important one – protect the artefact!"

"Nice work, Agent Zaiba! What did it say?"

"I'll tell you later." Zaiba glanced around to indicate all the others – now wasn't the time for sharing secrets, and Poppy nodded in understanding.

The History Club gathered in the Great Hall, which

had a high timber ceiling and wooden benches set out. The inn was L-shaped and the hall formed the shorter side that ran parallel to the cliff edge.

There was a small crowd in the room and everyone was murmuring among themselves as they waited for the event to begin. Zaiba spotted Keelie, the museum director, standing over to one side talking to a small group... It was the Richards! As Zaiba passed them she caught a snippet of their conversation.

"After the play yesterday, we are even more excited to finally see the artefact," Jacqueline enthused. "Such a brilliant idea to split the reveal into two events. How long exactly did you say this will take?"

"Oh, only half an hour. Though I'm sure there will be *lots* of questions to answer from the press," Keelie enthused. "I'm very proud of our little museum taking care of such an important artefact."

Zaiba noticed Leo roll their eyes at Sophie. It didn't seem like *they* were that excited for the reveal.

Jacqueline shot her children a stern look before plastering on a smile. "We can't stay for long – we have to set sail when the tide's in – but we are *so* looking forward to the reveal."

"Trust me, it's worth it." Keelie beamed before scurrying off to a little podium with a microphone.

Zaiba watched as the red-haired family sat on some seats next to a few of the museum staff who were all dressed in their costumes and excitedly chatting. The Tolworth Time Team that Zaiba had seen at the play yesterday were there again, sitting front and centre and wearing their club T-shirts proudly. Zaiba thought that Ms Talbot should get them some T-shirts made too. Poppy could be in charge of the design!

Zaiba had seen most of the audience at the play yesterday, however there were two men and a woman dressed in smart clothes sitting to the side of the podium who she hadn't seen before. When Zaiba looked closer at their lanyards, she could see the words 'Chesil Bay Council' written on them. Zaiba was impressed – if members of the council were here, it really was a big deal. Keelie was wearing a smart floral dress and earrings, obviously dressed to impress the news team.

Zaiba was pleased she'd worn her patterned top now!

Keelie turned around to speak to the two security guards Zaiba had seen earlier. They were guarding a door behind the podium, to the left of the hall.

"Who are they? They aren't in period dress," Mariam whispered in Zaiba's ear.

"They're the security, here to protect the artefact," Zaiba filled her in.

A small news team with a fancy camera and a presenter stood at the back of the room. Zaiba noticed that Connor had slipped into the hall and was edging his way in front of the camera. *Typical*.

Another guest caught her eye...

"I wonder why he's here?" Zaiba mumbled. Nudging Poppy, she pointed discreetly at the elderly gentleman they'd seen on the boat. He was dressed in yet another pinstriped suit and was squinting at Keelie. Zaiba noticed the shiny leather briefcase he'd had on the train was now balanced on his lap.

"Maybe he's an interested local?" Poppy suggested.

But Zaiba wasn't sure. "We saw him travelling down

on the train with us, which suggests he's not from here. And he didn't seem interested in the sunken shipwreck on the boat, did he? I really should find out his name..."

A high-pitched squeaking noise made everyone in the room cover their ears.

"Aargh, microphone interference," Ali winced.

"Oh, sorry, everyone, I'm not used to these," Keelie said, tapping the microphone and blushing. "I'm very happy and excited to have you all here today for the grand unveiling of the artefact found on the *Naseem* shipwreck." She looked around at the excited faces of the audience. "As you know, the artefact will be shipped out to Dispur Museum of Antiquities this evening. In the meantime, we are honoured they have let us reveal what it is. I would like to thank Sikora Security Solutions for protecting and overseeing the shipment of the artefact."

The two men guarding the door nodded at Keelie.

"Now, without further ado, I would like to show you all this wonderfully preserved, one-of-a kind object." Ms Talbot clapped her hands together. "It has been kept in one of the rooms behind me under lock and key.

It has to spend most of its time out of direct sunlight, to prevent tarnishing... Just give me a moment."

Everyone held their breath as Keelie opened the door. There seemed to be a corridor beyond but Zaiba couldn't see clearly. She heard Keelie open another door. This was it ... the moment she'd be proved right! There was a long silence and then...

"Nooooooooooooooooooooooooooooo!"

Zaiba felt her whole body go rigid and she had to fight her instincts to jump up.

Keelie came running out of the room, gasping. She grabbed one of the security guards by the shoulders, her eyes wide.

"It's gone!" she cried, her glance darting around the room. "The artefact's gone!"

"Calm down, Keelie. It can't possibly be gone, it was locked up in a safe!" The security guard's voice wavered.

But Keelie shook her head. "The safe is empty! And I've looked everywhere in the room but it's not there."

Keelie faced the seated audience and Zaiba felt like she was speaking directly to her. "It's been stolen!"

8

SCRAMBLE THROUGH THE MUSEUM

"Stolen?" cried a voice. Zaiba whirled round to see it was Jacqueline, clutching Sophie.

"The artefact's *gone*?" Connor hissed. His eyes were blazing.

"This is terrible!" one of the council members said.

Zaiba caught snippets of the fevered conversations. Everyone in the room had got to their feet, looking around suspiciously.

The History Club had surrounded Ms Talbot and were asking her a barrage of questions.

"Who stole it?" asked Ivy.

"What *is* the artefact, Ms?" asked Eva.

Jack wrung his hands. "Are we in danger?"

Ms Talbot's face had gone red and she was trying to hush the group. "I don't know, children. Just stay calm!"

Keelie was clearly in a state of shock, shaking and pacing the room. The news presenter was now in the middle of a crime scene – clearly making the most of it. She approached Keelie with the cameraman, holding out a microphone with a gleam in her eye. "Can you confirm what the artefact is exactly?" she asked, straightening her sharp suit for the camera.

The room suddenly went quiet as people waited to listen for Keelie's answer. Zaiba held her breath. Had she been right?

"It's … a priceless gold teapot from Assam!" Keelie wailed. "The handle is ebony, and the engravings are of elephants, which is so rare. It really is unique! Oh, and it's in almost perfect condition too after our restorations!"

Zaiba couldn't believe it – she'd been right! But any excitement she felt was quickly replaced by shock. The teapot had been stolen!

Ms Talbot stood to one side, weeping quietly into her

hands. "If only the History Club had a chance to witness it!" she was saying as Jessica placed a comforting hand round her shoulders. "This was our moment!"

Zaiba could understand Ms Talbot's sadness but she wasn't sure that the teapot's disappearance was *all* about them. Before she could say anything, the security guards pushed the reporter away and steered Keelie out of the Great Hall, into the corridor behind them.

"Nobody is to leave this room. Including the press!" a council member announced, before they followed Keelie into the corridor. Zaiba managed to gather herself, like a true detective, and watched everything with a steady gaze, mentally taking note.

"Did you hear that, Zaiba? You were right about the teapot!" Ali tugged on Zaiba's sleeve.

"I know, but that doesn't matter now," she said grimly. "A crime has been committed. Phase three of our mission isn't looking so good."

"Protect the artefact until it's shipped to Assam," Poppy repeated from memory.

"We still could... We just need to find it first." Zaiba

mustered her courage. "We can't give up hope!"

Zaiba stared at the doorway that Keelie had been led through, wondering where she'd been taken. Then she searched the crowd and noticed the Richards huddled together, deep in conversation. They looked worried, particularly Jacqueline. The museum staff were flitting about, though none of them seemed to know what they should be doing. The shock was etched on everyone's faces. Connor was already ordering staff around, bellowing out commands – and looking like he was enjoying the drama of it all.

Among the chaos there was another figure that caught Zaiba's attention. The elderly gentlemen. He was still sitting, leather briefcase now open on his lap as he sorted through it. What was he looking for? He was the calmest person in the room. Almost as if he'd been expecting the teapot to be stolen...

Zaiba's mind was buzzing but first she had to track down Keelie – and for that, she needed to ask her dad's permission. If she disappeared without telling him, he would worry. She scanned the group gathered around

Ms Talbot and caught her dad's eye. He and Jessica were busy calming down the members of the History Club. Zaiba motioned at the doorway and Hassan nodded. He'd seen his daughter in detective mode too many times now – he knew he couldn't stop her from tracking down a culprit!

With Poppy, Ali and Mariam following close behind, Zaiba slipped through the doorway. They found themselves in a small corridor that didn't look like the rest of the museum. It was more modern and had rooms either side with signs on that read, 'Head Curator', 'Overflow One' and 'Community Outreach Office'. All along the wall were paintings and huge prints of the coastline, neatly lined up and labelled with the artist's name.

"This must be where all the offices and storage rooms are for the museum," Zaiba noted.

The first door she encountered was the room that had contained the artefact. Or at least Zaiba deduced it was – since the door had been flung open! When she peered in, she saw upturned boxes, where Keelie must have searched for the teapot. They walked down the corridor until they heard hushed voices coming from behind a door labelled 'Museum Director'.

Zaiba reached to knock but hesitated for a moment, suddenly feeling doubtful.

"You can do this, Zai." Poppy put a hand on her shoulder.

"Yeah, Keelie needs the Snow Leopard Detective Agency," Ali agreed.

"I'm sure she'll want all the help she can get," Mariam said seriously.

Zaiba turned round and smiled at her team. "Thanks, guys."

She took a deep breath and knocked on the door. It was already ajar and the knocking pushed it fully open. Inside, Keelie and the two security guards were sitting at her desk, speaking quickly but in hushed tones. Keelie look up sharply and Zaiba noticed that her eyes were red-rimmed.

"Sorry, children. I can't answer any questions now," Keelie said, trying to force a smile.

"Actually, we've come to offer our help." Zaiba stepped forwards into the room. "My name is Zaiba and we are the Snow Leopard Detective Agency UK branch." She looked around proudly at her friends. "We'd like to help find the thief and the stolen artefact."

Keelie paused. "That's very kind of you ... but I have a security team here – Tom and Jo." Keelie gestured to the men sitting either side of her. Judging by the beads of sweat on their foreheads, Zaiba thought they must be every bit as agitated as Keelie.

"Perhaps we could all work together?" Zaiba offered. She was determined not to be shut out of this case!

The three adults looked at each other.

"I suppose ... it could be useful to have help while we do an initial sweep of the museum. Right, Jo?" the tallest guard said.

"Yes, and the council were clear they wanted this sorted with as little attention as possible. If Zaiba can keep people busy – I mean, be very useful while we carry out the search – we might not have to get the police involved," Jo replied.

Zaiba fought the urge to roll her eyes. These people just wanted to use them as a distraction while they searched the museum themselves! But at least they'd agreed to let them help.

"Where are the council members?" Zaiba asked quickly, before they had a chance to change their minds.

"They left through the back after giving us *quite* a talking to." Keelie rubbed her eyes. "Snow Leopard Detective Agency – we'll accept your help." Zaiba noticed the museum director was using the fake light-hearted voice that adults use when they try to pretend nothing's wrong. "It reminds me of when I was younger and me and my friends formed an 'archaeological dig' group. We used to find old pennies and things like that."

"We've solved a diamond theft," Poppy countered.

"And a poisoning," Mariam added, standing alongside Zaiba.

"Plus, a fake haunting by an evil property developer." Ali crossed his arms.

Zaiba couldn't help but smile at Keelie, Tom and Jo's shocked expressions.

"Uh, w-wow," Jo stammered. "That's quite a list."

Zaiba nodded. "Yes, and I'm sure we'll be adding 'solving a teapot heist' to it very soon. Now did you say you haven't called the police?"

"No. The council were quite clear on that," Keelie explained "The fewer people who know about this, the better. It doesn't look good for the museum or the council that we've lost such a precious item – and it's due to go back to Assam at 6:30 p.m. this evening, after the museum closes."

"It doesn't look good for your security firm either!" Mariam told Tom and Jo, blunt as ever.

Jo scowled. "I'm sure we'll find it."

"We just need to do a sweep of the museum," Tom added, fiddling with his tie.

"Great! An initial search sounds like a good plan." Zaiba looked at them expectantly and after a slight pause, both guards quickly hurried out the door.

Keelie sighed as she watched them go. "They came so highly recommended."

"It would be helpful to view any CCTV footage you

have of last night," Zaiba said. "And I also need to see that threatening note."

Keelie's eyes nearly popped out of her head. "How do you know about that?"

"Like I said," Zaiba said calmly, "we are professionals."

Keelie pulled open a desk drawer, and rummaged around inside. "I suppose there's no point in hiding it now. I received this two days ago. It was pushed under my office door." She handed over a torn scrap of paper. Just as Brenda had said, the message was scrawled in red pen.

"Did you know, people can be identified by their handwriting?" Ali said, peering at the note over Zaiba's shoulder.

"That could be why the writer deliberately used messy writing—so it can't be traced back to them," Zaiba pointed out, staring at the note. She took an empty plastic wallet that Keelie had lying on her desk and slid the note inside, then tucked the whole thing away in her backpack.

"Now, the CCTV..." Keelie swivelled towards her monitor.

Zaiba, Poppy, Ali and Mariam moved further into the

small office and crowded round the computer screen. "I just need to unlock my computer," Keelie said, trying different combinations. "Ugh, I can never remember passwords! It's why I usually have the same ones for everything."

Zaiba and Poppy's eyes met over the top of Keelie's head. Poppy's eyebrows were raised as if to say, *That doesn't sound very secure!* Zaiba was thinking the same thing. Then Keelie pulled out a small black diary from the top drawer of her desk and looked in the back page. Zaiba could see the word 'S4ILING' written in small letters at the top of the page. *Definitely not secure.*

Keelie typed in the password and pulled up the CCTV from the night before. She fast forwarded through it. The video showed the corridor with the office rooms and storage rooms. They could see Tom and Jo sitting on chairs outside the room where the artefact was. Then – all of a sudden – the footage cut off!

Keelie's hand flew to her mouth. "It just stops!"

"A malfunction?" Ali said.

"Or it's been tampered with." Zaiba narrowed her

eyes. "Any criminal would know to look for a password written in a diary. They could easily have found yours and used it to edit the CCTV footage through your computer."

Keelie put her head in her hands. "You're right. What was I thinking?"

Zaiba put a reassuring hand on Keelie's shoulder. "It's OK. When did you last see the artefact?"

Keelie thought for a moment. "Just before the play started. I checked on it inside the safe and locked it back up again. I'm sure of it."

"Then we know the crime was committed once the play had started and after the footage cut off." Zaiba checked the clock on the CCTV to confirm that the timings made sense. "If the safe and this room were locked this morning when you came to get the teapot, the criminals must have figured out the security code as well. They locked the door behind them to avoid arousing suspicion." Zaiba's mind was firing on all cylinders.

"I don't have that code written down anywhere, I promise!" Keelie was clearly really embarrassed by the password blunder. Honestly – adults! They could be so silly sometimes.

"The criminals must have figured it out another way." Zaiba scribbled notes in her detective book. "Do you have CCTV of the main gate at the front of the museum?"

Keelie nodded and pulled up a different window on her computer. The footage showed a black and white image of the outside courtyard and the main entrance to the museum compound. They watched as everyone arrived for the play – including their school group. Then, as the audience filed away to watch the show, the courtyard emptied and no one else entered or left until the play ended.

"What are you thinking, Zai?" Poppy asked, chewing her lip.

"We know the crime was committed during the play and no one else entered the museum compound in that time. Who does that leave as suspects?" Zaiba asked Poppy. They liked to test each other on their detective skills!

Poppy's eyes went wide. "Anyone in the museum – including all the audience at the play!"

"Bingo!" Zaiba clicked her fingers. "Come on, let's go back to the hall and see how Tom and Jo's search is going."

Zaiba let Keelie lead the way as she shut the office door behind them. They walked down the corridor back to the Great Hall. Zaiba was alarmed to hear that the room had become even noisier!

When they arrived, Zaiba understood why. Tom and Jo had made everyone get in a line and were searching through their bags, one by one. Everyone was complaining and grumbling as their possessions were taken out and examined.

"Well, that's a good way of annoying the whole room," Mariam said.

Tom quickly approached Keelie and took her aside. "We've searched everyone's bags and the teapot isn't here."

The thief must have stashed it somewhere, Zaiba thought.

"How could this have happened, Tom? That door and safe is locked with an alarm code only I know," Keelie said.

The crowd was getting agitated now, especially the

History Club. Waiting around wasn't part of their fun school trip. Zaiba felt a little bad for them but solving a crime was more important than another game of beach cricket!

"If you are the only one who knows the security code, why are *we* being held here?" came an accusing voice. It was Jacqueline, standing in line with her two children who were looking miserable and bored.

"What are you implying, Ms Richards?" Keelie asked through gritted teeth.

"At the very least, you should have been more careful. And perhaps *we* shouldn't be the ones being searched!" Jacqueline's eyes were burning with rage.

"How dare you accuse me!" Keelie shouted. "You're the antiques collector... I wouldn't be surprised if you had something to do with this!"

"Now, now," Ms Talbot piped up. "We're all history lovers here. I'm sure we're just upset about the teapot."

"Just how much *do* you love history?" Jacqueline turned on Ms Talbot. "Enough to steal a piece of it?"

"Hold on a minute!"

As the adults bickered uselessly, Zaiba scanned the room. The History Club children were in two camps – some finding their teacher's argument highly entertaining, the others hiding behind Jessica and Hassan. The news team were filming everything. A few of the living museum actors, including Connor, were watching their boss Keelie. Connor seemed agitated and was pacing around the room, while some of the staff seemed pleased to have a distraction from work.

But someone stood out to Zaiba. Everyone was displaying strong emotions – apart from one person. Once again, her gaze was drawn to the elderly gentleman in the pinstriped suit! He was still sitting, completely calm and watching the events unfold. Why wasn't he worried? She really wanted to question him, but she knew it wouldn't be easy. The man had been quick to dismiss her on the boat. Why would he listen to her now?

Zaiba had seen adults argue before and she knew that this could go on for a long time. And they didn't *have* time! The teapot needed to be found quickly, so it could be returned to its rightful home *that evening*. They now knew when the crime took place and they had a room full of suspects. There was really only one thing to do!

She took out her phone and quickly opened up the Snow Leopard Detective Agency UK branch group chat. It was usually just her, Poppy and Ali, but for this mission she had added Mariam's number too. She typed out a message and sent it off with a whooshing noise.

Major crime to investigate. Agents assemble!

9
SPLIT UP AND SPREAD OUT

Out in the courtyard, the team huddled to discuss their
first steps.

"I'd like to do a proper exploration of the entire
museum, before we do any questioning," announced
Zaiba, her mind buzzing. "All of our suspects are already
being held in the Great Hall. We might as well search
the museum while they're busy. If we're lucky, the teapot
might still be here somewhere. Everyone – keep a
lookout. Phase three has been updated – *find* and protect
the teapot so it can be returned to Assam tonight!"

Poppy, Ali and Mariam all gave a sharp nod.

The courtyard around them was deserted and there

was no sign of the woman with the placard – she had to be inside with everyone else.

Zaiba had brought her backpack with her. She took out a promotional leaflet that they'd been given on the tour. It had a few pages of historical information about the inn and, in the middle spread, a basic map of the museum buildings. Every detective needed a map!

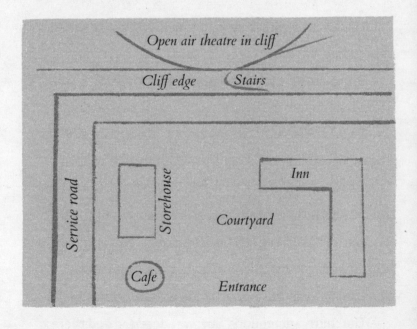

"We're here in the courtyard," Zaiba explained, drawing an X on part of the page. "Now we need to explore the main inn –" she pointed to her right – "which is the larger building we were just in. The old storehouse, the smaller building, is –" she pointed in the other direction – "to our left."

Ali was doing a slow 180-degree spin, peering at their surroundings.

"Ali, are you listening?" Zaiba asked.

Her little brother gave a sharp nod. "I'm trying to work out where Keelie's office is. I know we were in the inn building, but it felt like the corridor was longer than the perimeter of the building..."

Zaiba, Poppy and Mariam stared at him, confused.

"So, what you're saying is...?" Zaiba tried to figure it out.

"Follow me!" Ali took off towards the back of the inn. The girls followed hot on his trail and found themselves on the service road that ran behind the buildings.

Zaiba noted that the black security van was still parked in the same place. She narrowed her eyes.

She'd like to search in there too. The security team were present during the play and knew where the artefact had been stored... They couldn't be ruled out of the investigation.

"Ha! I knew it." Ali pointed at the back of the inn. Added on to the historical wooden building was a modern extension. "The offices and storerooms aren't part of the original inn. They were built on later."

"Good work, Ali!" Zaiba hastily sketched out the shape of the extension on to her map.

"OK, so we know the layout of the building. Now what?" Mariam stood with her fists on her hips.

Zaiba chewed her lip. "The museum is big. I think we'll have to follow Eden Lockett's golden rule number six, which is...?" Zaiba looked at Poppy expectantly. They both loved the Eden Lockett books and had memorized all the rules long ago!

Poppy screwed up her face, thinking hard. Then she clicked her fingers. "I've got it. *When you have to cover a lot of ground, split up and spread out.*"

"Bingo!" Zaiba high-fived her best friend.

"How many of those golden rules are there anyway?" Mariam screwed up her nose. "There must be one that's the most important."

"There is," Zaiba said, her eyes twinkling. "Golden rule number one!"

"Which is?" Ali ventured.

"You'll have to read the books to find out." Zaiba winked, before getting back to business. "Mariam — you and I will take the main inn building. Poppy — you and Ali explore the old storehouse. Take pictures of anything strange and we'll report back here in fifteen. Have you all got your phones charged?" It was always vital to have the right equipment. Everyone took out their devices and gave a sharp nod. "Cool! Let's go."

Poppy led Ali off to the warehouse, trying to reassure him as he complained about having to search somewhere that might include spiders. Ali *did not* like spiders, but after his help in the case of the missing diamonds, he was getting braver at facing them.

Zaiba and Mariam made their own way to the office block. Since they'd just had a tour of the public rooms – at the front of the inn – it seemed sensible to start at the back.

As they walked round the side of the office block, Zaiba spotted a fire exit. The door had been left slightly open and Zaiba noticed some footprints in the shingle. They led from the doorway out into the open space between the building and the service road.

"Footprints!" Mariam cried, noticing the same thing. "Maybe it was the criminal?"

Zaiba followed the footprints across to a parking bay, where they were replaced by tyre tracks. "No," she sighed. "Keelie said the council members left her office before we got there, remember? There are three sets here, two larger for the men and one smaller for the woman. These are their footprints. But at least they left the fire exit open for us!"

Zaiba retrieved a large stone from the car park and used it to prop open the fire exit. "Now we have access through the back to investigate." She smiled, heading in.

Mariam hesitated. "Are you sure it's OK for us to go in?" she said, her voice wavering.

"I'm sure. Keelie said we're allowed to help. Keep your eyes peeled for anything dropped on the floor, marks on the walls, items that have been disturbed ... that kind of thing."

Zaiba had opened the door on to another corridor that looked *very* similar to the one Keelie's office was in. White walls, a blue scratchy carpet and bright overhead lights.

Mariam tried one door handle that was marked 'Archive 3a' but it was locked.

"Makes sense," Zaiba reasoned. "This must be where the museum items that aren't on display are stored." Silently, they moved on to the next door, marked 'Archive 3b'. Zaiba tested the door handle and it opened. *Result!*

The room was dark inside. Zaiba felt on the wall for a light switch and flicked it on, revealing a white room lined with shelves. To the left were huge cabinets and drawers filled with various artefacts. Other objects were out on a table, surrounded by brushes and cleaning fluids. The room smelled of dust and chemicals, which made Zaiba's nose itch.

"Archive 3b appears to be where they restore the artefacts before they go into the museum." Zaiba made a quick voice recording on her phone.

"Look at all those files in the bookcases – they are chock full." Mariam grimaced. "Imagine having to sort through those."

"Luckily we don't have to. Nothing seems amiss in here." Zaiba took a quick snap of the room before flicking the light off and shutting the door.

There were two more rooms that were similar – storing various items and equipment for the museum. Everything looked normal. Well, normal for a museum – one room had two skulls on a table!

Just as they were about to leave another fairly boring office, Zaiba heard movement in the corridor. "Wait!" she whispered.

Zaiba opened the door a fraction and peered out. She was just in time to catch the flash of a pinstriped suit walking into the office opposite them before the door closed. That man again!

"Follow my lead," Zaiba instructed. With Mariam behind her, she walked straight out of the office and into the one opposite, swinging open the door.

"Dad?" she called, looking around. "Oh, so sorry. I didn't see you in here! I was looking for my dad."

"Yeah, we thought we saw him come in here," Mariam said, playing along.

The elderly man was staring at a wall poster. He slowly turned round, his eyes narrowed. "You!" He pointed at Zaiba. "I met you on the boat."

"That's right," Zaiba said, keeping her head held high. "I'm Zaiba. What's your name?"

The man regarded her for a while before answering. "My name is Christophe Pinel. You can call me Mr Pinel."

Zaiba hadn't noticed before, but now she could detect a slight French accent in his voice.

"What are you doing in here?" Mariam asked. "You were supposed to stay in the hall!"

Oof, a bit too forward! Zaiba thought. *Though she has a point.*

Mr Pinel immediately bristled. "Nothing that

concerns you, mademoiselle. And I could ask you the same thing!" He strode out the door.

"Well, he was rude," Mariam commented.

Zaiba walked over to the wall where Mr Pinel had been standing. The poster he'd been studying was an old map of the museum – though it was more detailed than the one in the leaflet. There were measurement guides down each side and in swirling script the map read: Chesil Bay Inne, 1750.

Zaiba's eyes widened. "These are the original plans for the inn! Remember Brenda/Marie the Barmaid? She said it had burned down, and then was rebuilt? This must be what it looked like before they rebuilt it." She got out the map in her leaflet and held it next to the detailed one on the wall, comparing the two. "Hmmm, that's strange."

"What is?" Mariam came alongside.

"This tiny room here." Zaiba pointed at the map on the wall. There was a small, very faint square room marked on the map at the back of the inn building – right next to where the new office addition had been built. "This room isn't marked on the map in the leaflet, but it looks like it was part of the main inn. I wonder why..."

"Maybe they never rebuilt that room?" Mariam mused.

"We can ask Keelie later. Right now I think we should reconvene with Ali and Poppy to see what they've found," Zaiba said. "Ali will definitely want to take a look at this missing room." She snapped a photo of the plan on her phone. Then she marked the missing room on her map, before packing it away.

With a final scan of the place, the girls exited and made their way back to the courtyard. The initial exploration was complete. The mysterious extra room on the old map they found, plus Mr Pinel roaming around when he'd been told to stay in the hall with the other guests... These were both definite leads. It was time to share their findings!

10
THE MISSING ROOM

"Three small spiders, two big ones and *eight* giant webs!" Ali announced as they joined back up in the courtyard. He shuddered and wiped his arms, just to make sure there were no spiders lurking there.

"Apart from the spiders ... any leads?" Zaiba asked Poppy who was giggling at Ali.

"Not really," her friend said. "It looked like a normal museum exhibit. Glass cabinets with artefacts in, old oil lamps, picks and shovels... No priceless gold teapots."

"Don't worry. No clue is also a clue. And we've something to show you." Zaiba felt her eyes shining.

"Well... We have something to *not* show you,"

Mariam corrected her.

Poppy and Ali looked bewildered.

"Just follow us." Zaiba led the way back to the offices built on to the back of the inn. They crept in through the fire-escape door, down the corridor and round to the second corridor where Keelie's office and the room that had held the teapot were.

"First of all," Zaiba began, "we saw Mr Pinel – the man in the pinstriped suit – snooping around."

"That man again!" Poppy said.

Zaiba nodded. "I know. There's something suspicious about him. He didn't explain why he was here and wouldn't answer any of our questions. We followed him into an office where there was a plan of the inn dating from 1750 hanging on the wall. And there was something really odd about it."

She pulled the leaflet out of her backpack and held it open at the map for Poppy and Ali to see. "There was a really small room, drawn in here." Zaiba jabbed her finger at the map, where she'd faintly traced the missing room. She took out her phone and showed them the photo of the plan.

Zaiba marched down the corridor, counting doors, until she came to the final door in the corridor. "This is the room where the artefact was being stored. The faint room we saw on the original map is supposed to be next to it..."

"But this is where the corridor ends. The room isn't there," Poppy breathed.

"I reckon they just never rebuilt it," Mariam said.

"Maybe they ran out of space?" Ali said.

Zaiba hesitated. Perhaps they were right. So, why did she get a niggling sense that it was important somehow?

Poppy must have seen the look on her face. "It might be nothing, but we can't discount it as a clue. Right, Zaiba?"

Zaiba grinned at her best friend. "Right! Now I think it's time we looked at the crime scene. Remember not to touch anything because we might need to take fingerprints later."

Before stepping inside the room where the artefact had been stored, Zaiba examined the alarm system. It was a square panel on the wall next to the door with numbered buttons. It looked old and worse for wear.

Some of the numbers had completely rubbed off!

When she'd peeked in earlier, Zaiba had only noticed the chaos that Keelie had left behind from scouring the room for the teapot. Now, with the main lights on, she realized it wasn't a storage room or an office at all.

"Wow, this room is fancy!" Poppy said, looking around. "Look at this wood panelling. Very classy."

Poppy was right. The room had shiny panelled walls instead of bare brick like the other offices. The furniture was also very grand, with a big wooden table in the middle and polished oak chairs surrounding it.

"This looks like the meeting room at my mum's work," Mariam observed, gesturing at a water jug on a side cabinet. "Maybe this is where Keelie holds important meetings."

"And important teapots," Ali added.

Zaiba walked around the room. There were pretty decorations including a model ship in a glass bottle and a big crystal bowl full of intricate shells. Set within a chest of drawers was a safe, with the door open. It was empty. That must have been where the teapot was kept.

She took out her phone and snapped a few pictures, so they had a record of exactly how the room had been left. Satisfied that they'd searched the crime scene thoroughly, she turned to the others, smiling. "Since we're in a meeting room, I think we should have a meeting!"

Zaiba cleared away the upturned boxes and files from the large table. As they'd been moved by Keelie in her search for the teapot, it was unlikely that they'd need to be dusted for the criminal's fingerprints. Then she sat down at one of the oak chairs with Poppy, Ali and Mariam joining her.

Zaiba unpacked her notebook and pen. "It's time to make a list of possible suspects and motives," she said, drawing a table on the open page.

Poppy clapped her hands together. "Yes, this is my favourite part!"

"OK, first... Who was at the museum last night at the time of the crime?"

Zaiba started a long list.

History Club members
Ms Talbot
Mum and Dad
The Richards
Museum staff and actors (including Connor)
Protestor woman
Keelie
Tolworth Time Team

"Who on earth are they?" Ali asked pointing at the last name on the group.

"They're a history club like us. You know the group in matching T-shirts? But they were sitting near the front of the stage for the whole play. Everyone would have seen someone get up from their group and sneak off."

"What about Christophe Pinel?" Poppy raised a finger. "We saw him at the end of the play but couldn't be sure if he was there at the beginning."

Zaiba nodded. "True. That makes him high on our list of suspects." She quickly added him to the list. "Now to narrow it down. Who could have known the security code to get into the room and the safe where the teapot was being held? Keelie said she uses the same password for everything. I'm willing to bet it's the same for number codes too."

Zaiba tapped her pen to the page and then wrote:

Suspect	Motive and Opportunity
Keelie	Knew code. Wanted to drum up attention for the museum?
Tom and Jo, security guards	Could have spied on Keelie to get the code. Sell the teapot for money?

"You don't seem so sure of those suspects." Ali watched his sister. "You're doing that thing where you screw up your nose."

Zaiba sighed. "You're right. Those motives don't

seem strong enough to me. Keelie wouldn't want to ruin the reputation of her museum, and neither would the security guards for their business."

"What about any of the actors?" Poppy suggested. "They might have overseen Keelie putting the code in too?"

"Good idea." Zaiba scribbled on the page.

Actors – Connor	Didn't like being questioned. Enjoys the limelight of having more tourists/press at the museum. Threatening to the other actor who broke character. Knows his way around museum.

"Now, suspects who didn't have the security code but are still suspicious," Zaiba said, knowing exactly who she wanted to jot down.

Christophe Pinel	Skulking around the offices when he was told to stay in the hall. Wasn't shocked when the teapot was announced missing. Came with his briefcase full of equipment. Can't be placed at the play during time period when crime was committed.
Protestor	Always at the museum and doesn't want the artefact to leave Chesil Bay. Wasn't at the play – whereabouts unknown during that time.

The Richards	Love history/antiques collectors. Jacqueline very intense. Were at the play but sat at the back.

Zaiba clicked her pen shut. That was a good place to start. "Any one of these suspects could also be responsible for the threatening note. I'd like to speak to Tom and Jo, to find out exactly what happened yesterday evening when they were 'guarding' the artefact." Zaiba packed away her things.

"So, are they suspects or are we working with them?" asked Mariam.

"Good question." Zaiba thought back to Eden Lockett in *The Cottage on the Cliff*. Eden had to stay at the cottage with the owner during her investigation, despite thinking that he was a suspect. Sometimes you had to keep suspects closer than you'd like...

"Both," Zaiba decided. "We want them to think we're working together while we do this initial questioning."

"Questioning without letting them *know* we're questioning them." Poppy wiggled her eyebrows.

"Sneaky, I like it!"

Zaiba laughed. Questioning people was Poppy's speciality. She was very good at acting and had a way of getting people to trust her.

"Why don't you take the lead on this one, Pops?" Zaiba suggested.

"With pleasure!" Poppy smiled.

Zaiba could just make out a hushed conversation coming from the hall next to the offices. What was going on there? Exploring the museum meant she hadn't been able to keep tabs on the guests. At least they were all in one place. She was itching to question them, but she tried to stop her racing thoughts and focus on the moment. First things first. She needed answers from Tom and Jo.

11
SIKORA SECURITY SOLUTIONS

The sun was directly overhead in the courtyard as Zaiba, Ali, Poppy and Mariam stepped out in search of the two security guards. Seagulls swirled overhead and beyond the cliff edge Zaiba could hear the faint sound of waves crashing, reminding her just how close they were to the sea.

Zaiba had poked her head into the hall to see if Tom and Jo were still there, but Keelie had told her they'd gone back to their van to collect some equipment. Luckily Zaiba knew exactly where that van was – parked on the service road that ran round the outside of the two museum buildings.

"Hey, look, it's the Richards kids." Poppy pointed.

Sophie and Leo were sitting on a bench in the courtyard, their red hair even brighter in the sunlight. They were both hunched over a book. Leo was scribbling away with a pencil while Sophie pointed at something on the page.

The twins were sitting next to the path Zaiba needed to take, so it only seemed polite to say hello as they passed by. Zaiba was on a mission but she wasn't rude.

"Hi, again!" She smiled at the siblings, who looked up from their activity and blinked in the sunlight.

"Hey," Sophie said. "It was getting boring in there, so we slipped out."

"I don't think we properly met but I'm Zaiba. This is Poppy, Ali and Mariam." Zaiba pointed at each of them in turn.

"I'm Sophie and this is Leo. But good luck getting them to notice you. Once they get started on these puzzles, it's hard to snap them out of it."

Ali leaned over to look at the page Leo was still studying intently. After a few moments, Ali suddenly snapped his fingers together. "Nine!" he announced, smiling proudly.

Leo gave a low whistle. "Impressive! Bet you can't solve *this* one as fast, though." They pointed to the page. "Took me a while, but I've just got it."

"Um, what's going on?" Poppy looked from Ali to Leo to Zaiba. But even Zaiba was clueless.

"It's a logic puzzle, and it's really hard!" Ali explained, gesturing to the book. "This one is a number sequence. I love doing these!"

"We spend a lot of time sailing on the boat, so Leo and I do these logic puzzle books to pass the time," Sophie explained. "I guess most teenagers don't do number pattern puzzles for fun..."

"Being different is a good thing!" Poppy said. "And you guys are collectors, right? I think that's really cool."

Zaiba looked at her best friend and instantly smiled. Poppy was great at making people feel good about themselves!

"Ha, thanks. Though I don't think many of my mates think our collection of old maps, crockery and teapots are that cool," Leo said, still focused on the puzzles.

"I love teapots!" Zaiba gushed. "I would have loved to

have seen the one that's been stolen. It's due to be sent back to Assam this evening, you know?"

"Yeah. Well, I'm sure they'll find it." Sophie said, though she didn't seem that bothered.

Zaiba felt a twist of frustration in her stomach. How could you not care that a priceless artefact was missing?

"Was that your boat I saw out in the harbour?" Poppy asked. "I liked the blue rowboat it had attached to it. It's like a toy boat! What do you use it for?"

"Yeah, it's ours. The rowboat is for getting to shore in difficult-to-land places, but we don't really use it." Sophie shifted in her seat awkwardly. "Anyway, we'd better go back inside."

The twins quickly got up and disappeared into the inn. Zaiba kicked herself – they had asked too many questions! No one liked feeling they were being interrogated.

"I wanted to have another go at those puzzles," Ali moaned, watching them go.

"There's no time for puzzles." Zaiba wagged her finger. "We need to go and interview the Sikoras."

"I'm too hot and sweaty," Mariam groaned, hiding in the shade under an awning on the inn building.

Zaiba softened. Not everyone was used to detective work – it was very tiring! She filled up her water bottle at the little fountain in the courtyard and brought it back to Mariam. "Here, drink this. You and Ali stay here in the courtyard while Poppy and I go question Tom and Jo. Keep an eye out for anyone moving around suspiciously. We know our thief is still here and I don't want them to move the artefact right under our noses!"

"You do realize I'm only one point three metres." Ali gestured to his frame and Zaiba giggled. "How am I supposed to stop a thief if one walks past?"

"Any problem, come and find us." Zaiba patted Ali's head.

"Yeah, don't go flinging yourself at any criminals while we're gone," Poppy said, laughing. Ali stuck his tongue out at them as they walked away, before joining Mariam in the shade to keep watch.

Tom and Jo were digging through the contents of their van when Zaiba and Poppy found them. They had opened the back doors and were on their hands and knees, looking through various crates and bags.

"Um, hi. Can we speak to you for a minute?" Zaiba called, standing at the rear of the van.

Tom lifted his head up from his search and flinched slightly when he saw Zaiba and Poppy looking in at them. "Oh, Zaiba. Yes, but it will have to be quick."

"Of course. What are you looking for?" Poppy stepped forwards and smiled as sweetly as possible.

"A fingerprint-detecting black light for searching the room," Jo sighed.

Zaiba mentally added *fingerprint-detecting black light* to her list of must-have detective equipment.

"Speaking of the room, were you two up watching it all night? You must be tired," Poppy said.

Zaiba wished she could whip out her phone and record what Tom and Jo said in reply but that would only put them on their guard. She'd have to write her notes up later! She leaned in slightly, waiting for their response.

"I suppose it has been a long night ... and day."
Tom rubbed his face with his hands.

"So, when everyone was watching the play yesterday
evening, you were both watching the room. The *whole*
time?" Poppy pushed again, trying to seem casual.

"Yes, we were there the whole time. It's our job."
Jo answered this time, a little gruffly. "Though there
was one incident during the play. We heard loud
banging so Tom went to investigate while I stayed."

"Oh, really." Zaiba stepped forward, trying not to look
too excited at this fresh information. "How long would
you say Tom was gone for?"

"A few minutes."

"Fifteen minutes."

The Sikoras answered at the same time. There was an
awkward pause.

Zaiba narrowed her eyes. Those were two wildly
different answers. They weren't telling her something.
Zaiba let the silence sit for a while, watching the two
men's faces turn bright red.

Tom spoke first. "It was fifteen minutes. I couldn't

find the source of the banging anywhere. Look, I know I shouldn't have left my post for so long but Jo was there the whole time!"

Jo shifted uncomfortably and let out a sigh. "Actually, when Tom was off investigating the banging, I heard some shouting. It sounded really aggressive and I was worried about Tom, so ... I left to go and find him. I suppose that's the problem working with your spouse. You worry about them more than you would a business partner. It turns out that the shouting was just that actor, Connor, warming up for his monologue."

"Wait, you're married?" Poppy squealed. "A married security team! That's so cute."

Tom and Jo did *not* look pleased to be called cute.

"Back to the matter in hand." Zaiba regained her composure. "The room was actually left unguarded for around fifteen minutes?"

"Yes, from around 5:45 to 6:00 p.m.," Jo confirmed. "When I got back the security alarm was still set so I didn't think to check the room. Then Tom got back, and I didn't mention I'd left. I'm sorry..."

Jo looked really guilty and Zaiba knew he wouldn't make the same mistake again. Something popped into her mind. "You wouldn't have had anything to do with the missing CCTV footage, would you, Jo?"

"No, of course not!" Jo looked outraged, but Zaiba had met very good liars before.

"You do realize that leaving your posts is highly suspicious?" Zaiba was getting firm in her questioning now. "You could be making up this story about the banging to cover for the crime!"

Zaiba wasn't usually so hard on potential suspects but she thought the security guards ought to know better. Leaving your post was *very* unprofessional. The teapot would still be safe if they hadn't left it unattended!

"I know, I know," Jo babbled on. "But I promise I'm telling the truth."

"And with the threatening note that Keelie received, you should have *doubled* your security," Zaiba pressed on. "Did you not take it seriously?"

Tom scoffed, "Oh, come on. *You'd better keep the artefact safe, who knows what could happen?* It's hardly threatening."

"It was enough to scare Keelie into hiring you!" Poppy retorted, dropping her 'nice guy' act.

Both men went quiet and looked down at their shoes.

Zaiba took out the map with her extra markings on it and showed it to the Sikoras. "Where would you say you heard the thud noise coming from?"

Reluctantly, Tom studied the map for a while. "It sounded like it was coming from here." He pointed to the back entrance to the office block.

"Thanks for your help." Zaiba folded the map up and gestured to Poppy to move out. Tom was still giving Jo a very hard stare and she figured the couple needed some time to discuss Jo's revelation.

Back in the courtyard, Ali and Mariam sat on a bench while Zaiba and Poppy paced. It helped them to think, plus it was what all the great detectives did on TV when they were working something out.

"So, we know there were mysterious banging noises from near the office block entrance," Zaiba pondered.

"We know the room was unguarded, giving the criminal a chance to get in, steal the teapot *and* leave again, locking the room behind them," Poppy added, pacing in the opposite direction.

"We know the crime happened between 5:45 p.m. and 6:00 p.m.!" Ali added, shading his face from the sun.

"And we know that's it's *really* hot out here and I'm *really* thirsty," Mariam groaned, fanning her face.

Zaiba stopped pacing and opened up her backpack.

"Mariam's right, we need to stay hydrated and energized." She got out a bottle of water and some cereal bars.

"Great, food helps me think better." Poppy grinned, eagerly accepting a snack.

As her team recharged their energy levels, Zaiba thought hard about something that Jo had said. He'd heard aggressive shouting... She wondered if it was the same aggressive shouting that she'd heard down on the beach. But that had sounded as if it came from inside the cliffs.

Had it been Connor too? If so, then how had he got into the caves?

12
THE NEXT LEAD

5:45 p.m. to 6:00 p.m. Just fifteen short minutes, but in that time a priceless historical artefact had been stolen.

Zaiba tapped her foot on the courtyard ground and noticed the shadows of the benches had moved. Time was passing and they still had a list of suspects they needed to investigate. Plus, the museum would have to let the guests leave soon, meaning the criminal would be able to get away and the artefact could be lost forever.

"Let's look at our list of suspects," Zaiba announced, once again getting out her crime-solving notebook.

"We know the criminal has to be someone who was in the museum at the time of the play. That includes everyone in the audience. Did we notice anyone sneaking off?" Zaiba looked at the list of names, writing down who she could be sure didn't leave the play at any point.

- Spotted at the play (has an alibi).
- The History Club – sitting in front.
- Ms Talbot – very into the play and made lots of loud gasps, was there throughout!
- Mum and Dad – sitting next to us.
- Tolworth Time Club – sitting near the front of the stage the whole time.

Zaiba tapped her pencil against her chin. "I saw the Richards there too."

"Write them down," Poppy encouraged. "Also write down the actors who were in the play."

Zaiba nodded.

- Richards family – sitting at the back.
- Living Museum actors.

"Urgh, do you remember when Connor did that *looonnggg* speech at the end?" Mariam rolled her eyes.

"But he wasn't in the first act when the crime took place." Poppy seemed excited. "He could have done it!"

Zaiba held up a hand. "Let's not get carried away. Jo stumbled across Connor rehearsing during the time the room was unguarded. So, he can't have stolen the teapot himself."

"The shouting could have been a distraction to draw the guards away?" Poppy suggested.

"That's true. He could have an accomplice." Zaiba nodded. She wrote down, 'Accomplice?'

"And what about that woman who was protesting outside?" Ali pointed at the crate she had been standing on, which was currently empty. "She wasn't at the play. She could have stolen the teapot."

Zaiba nodded along as she wrote, adding a few more names.

- Not at the play (no alibi = high priority suspects).

- Connor — seen by Jo when the crime took place. Working with someone else?
- Keelie — not there (probably working, no convincing motive for stealing the teapot).
- Christophe Pinel — seen at the end of the play, where was he during?
- Protesting woman — not at the play at all, has opportunity and motive (wants the teapot to stay in the town).

Zaiba, Poppy, Ali and Mariam stared at the list of potential suspects. Zaiba's brain felt muddled. She was following the correct procedure for an investigation, just like she always did. Look for clues in the vicinity, question people present and narrow down a list of suspects. So why did everything seem so confusing?

She sat on the bench and rested her chin on her hands. Poppy sat down next to her, putting a hand on her back.

"What's up, Zai?" Poppy stroked her back. "You've got a list of leads here. I thought you'd be happy."

"I know. But I can't shake one thing from my mind."

"What is it?"

"I just keep thinking – how did an artefact get stolen from a safe in a room that was locked with an alarm? Somebody would have heard the alarm go off if the door was opened. The only way someone could do it without setting off the alarm was if they had the code. But the people with access to the code don't have a motive!" Zaiba kicked her foot against the ground.

"It could have been smuggler ghosts?" Ali joked, trying to lighten the mood.

"I think you need to take it one step at a time." Mariam came and sat next to Zaiba. "When you solved the poisoning case, you did everything in order. You followed whatever lead you had, rather than trying to jump to the end and guess the culprit straight away."

Poppy looked at Mariam wide-eyed. "Wow, Mariam. That's very nice of you to say."

Mariam shrugged, trying to act cool. "It just makes sense. That's all."

Zaiba took a deep breath and squeezed both Poppy

and Mariam to her. "Thank you, you're the best team ever!"

"What about me?" Ali complained.

"You too, Ali." Zaiba grinned. "And Mariam's right.
I just have to follow the next lead. Right now, that's
Keelie — we know she had the codes. Let's find out
where she was during the show."

The museum director was back in her office, poring
over the CCTV yet again and desperately looking for
clues. When Zaiba knocked on the door, Keelie sat up
hopefully, her eyes red and puffy.

"Ah, Zaiba! Please tell me you've found the teapot!"
Keelie cried out, grabbing Zaiba's hands.

"Uh, no, but—" Zaiba tried to free herself from
Keelie's grip.

"But you have a suspect?" Keelie's eyes were wide.

"We have a few leads..." Zaiba was being vague in
order to protect her theories, but Keelie just fell back in
her chair, deflated.

"I think it's time I called the police. It's getting late and the teapot could be anywhere by now." Keelie smoothed down her hair. "I had to fight so hard to have it returned to its place of origin. And now the people of Assam won't even be able to see it."

"Please, Keelie, don't worry!" Poppy came forward now, trying to reassure the museum director.

"Yeah, we'll find it," Ali chimed in.

"The Snow Leopard Detective Agency UK branch has never left a case unsolved," Zaiba assured her.

There was a gasp from the doorway behind them. Zaiba whirled round just in time to see Mr Pinel, backing out of the room. *He knows we're investigating! And he sounded worried...* Zaiba thought.

"He did knock but none of you heard," Mariam said to the shocked faces. She'd been standing at the back of the room closest to the door.

"Ali and Mariam, follow him!" Zaiba said.

Ali saluted her and so did Mariam.

"Yes, ma'am!" Mariam said.

"Understood!" Ali added.

"Just one last thing," Zaiba instructed, looking from

one face to the other. "Don't let him see you tracking him. Stay absolutely invisible then let me know where he goes."

As they ran – quietly – down the corridor, Zaiba turned back to the director's office. "Can't you tell me anything about what you've found out?" Keelie begged Zaiba and Poppy. "It's been two hours, you must have found *something*."

Zaiba nodded and took a deep breath. "We know the artefact was stolen between 5:45 p.m. and 6:00 p.m. as the room was left unguarded. Jo thought Tom was in danger, so he went off to help him. He admitted it all to us."

Keelie's face went through a curious mix of emotions: shock, outrage, anger and finally determination. "That's when the play was on. I was outside with Faye, trying to convince her to put down that awful sign." Keelie looked out of her office window.

"Is Faye the woman who protests?" Poppy asked.

"Yes, we went to school together. I was trying to explain to her why the artefact should go back to India where it belongs." Zaiba followed Keelie's eyeline and realized she must be looking to where the shipwreck was. Where all this began.

Keelie and Faye both had an alibi – they were outside in the courtyard when the crime took place. Since they were sort-of enemies, they wouldn't be likely to give each other a false alibi to help each other out.

Suddenly, Zaiba remembered something she'd wanted to ask Keelie for a while. She got out her map and unfolded it on the desk.

"Keelie, we found an old map on the wall in one of the offices and it showed a faint outline of a tiny room just *here*." She pointed to the map. "But the room doesn't exist where it's supposed to at the end of the corridor, plus there's no records of it on the modern maps."

Keelie looked perplexed. "I have to admit, Zaiba, this is the first I'm hearing of a tiny room. I suppose I didn't examine the old plans quite as thoroughly as you..." She looked embarrassed and was avoiding Zaiba's gaze.

They were interrupted by another knock at the office door. Jacqueline Richards was standing there, in heels and a matching red leather handbag. "Excuse me," she said, her hands on her hips. "We need to leave the harbour while the tide's in."

"I bet that handbag is vintage," Poppy whispered longingly.

Keelie narrowed her eyes at the newcomer. Clearly she hadn't forgotten how Jacqueline had accused her earlier. "You'll just have to wait like everyone else!"

Jacqueline looked like she was going to argue but she must have seen the anger on Keelie's face. "Very well. But unless I am actually *under arrest* I will not be held here for much longer." Jacqueline left the room, slamming the door behind her and causing the paintings in the corridor to rattle on their fittings.

"Be careful!" Keelie called after her. She looked at Zaiba and Poppy apologetically. "I'm going to have to call the police. Hopefully they can sort this all out so we can get everyone home – and get the teapot on its way to Assam tonight!"

Poppy reached out and squeezed Zaiba's hand. They were running out of time. If the police got here, they'd take over the investigation!

But Zaiba's mind was on a different matter. Keelie had

mentioned the tides on their boat tour yesterday too. They were clearly important to the area and Zaiba had a feeling they were important to this case.

As Keelie dialled the police, Zaiba went to the office door and peered out.

She saw Jacqueline walking to the end of the corridor towards the door that connected the offices to the Great Hall. She paused briefly at the end of the corridor and adjusted the last painting on the wall, before heading back into the hall. It must have fallen when Jacqueline had slammed the door.

Zaiba took Poppy's hand and led her down the corridor. The large painting was of a ship on a stormy sea.

"It looks just like Chesil Bay." Zaiba pointed at the coastline in the painting. "And those must be the smugglers' ships coming in to dock."

The colours and lines of the painting were so vivid, it looked like the waves could splash right off the painting on to the floor!

"I didn't notice that before," Poppy said, staring at the wall.

"Hmmm..." Zaiba was forming an idea and it required someone with knowledge of the coast. "I want to speak to Faye to confirm Keelie's alibi. Plus, she might have seen something if she's out in the courtyard all day. I hope she's there now."

They ran back along the office corridor and out of the fire exit, working their way to the courtyard. There were more people outside now.

Jessica was doing her best to keep the History Club entertained. She'd drawn a big hopscotch in chalk on the ground and everyone was taking turns. Trust an art teacher to always keep a ready supply of chalk!

Hassan beckoned Zaiba and Poppy over and spoke to them in hushed tones.

"Any luck finding the teapot?" he said, looking from face to face. "Everyone's getting restless."

"Not yet but we're closing in on it," Zaiba said confidently.

"Look, Zai – Faye's back!" Poppy pointed to the spot where the woman stood, still holding her sign but looking a bit dejected.

"Gotta go, Dad," Zaiba said before they shot off across the square. As they crossed the courtyard, Zaiba kept her eyes peeled for Connor but the pretend smuggler was nowhere to be seen.

Faye seemed a little frightened to see Zaiba and Poppy running towards her, but she didn't leave her DIY podium.

"Faye!" Zaiba panted, slightly out of breath. "Can we ask you some questions?"

"I guess, sure," Faye replied nervously. "About my protest?"

"Sort of." Poppy smiled.

"I was wondering if you spoke to Keelie yesterday?" Zaiba asked as calmly as possible. She didn't want to give anything away.

"Yes, I did. She came out once the play had started." Faye sighed. "She was trying to convince me *again* why she's sending the teapot away and ruining our chances of boosting tourism. And now it's been stolen! I knew it wasn't safe with Keelie." She shook her head. "I should have done more."

"What do you mean?" Zaiba pressed.

"Oh, just that, uh — I wouldn't trust Keelie with guarding anything," Faye said. "Do you know, she uses the same number for her phone PIN code as her credit card? She actually told me!"

"Even I know that isn't a good idea," Poppy exclaimed.

"Well, thank you for your help," Zaiba said, pulling Poppy away. "For what it's worth, I don't think you need a teapot to bring more tourists to the area. Chesil Bay is great!"

"It is the best place in the country, in my opinion," Faye said proudly.

Zaiba and Poppy thanked Faye and walked away. The museum director's alibi was genuine, *and* something that Faye said was sticking in Zaiba's mind — "I should have done more" to protect the teapot. *More of what?* Zaiba wondered. She pulled out her phone and quickly typed a message in the Snow Leopard Detective Agency group chat.

Come to back of the inn. Need to share findings. We're close!

13
LET'S DO THIS!

"I've called you back here because the courtyard is too busy now. Too many eyes and ears," Zaiba explained.

They were behind the main inn building, near to the office block and crouched behind a parked car. It wasn't the top-secret HQ Zaiba would have hoped for but when you were out in the field investigating, sometimes you had to improvise.

"Agents Ali and Mariam – where did Mr Pinel go after he left Jacqueline's office?" Zaiba asked.

"He went back to the courtyard and straight up to Dad. We heard him asking if Dad had any famous relatives," Ali told them.

"Yeah, the questions were strange," Mariam added. "Then he just went and sat in the shade, doing his snort laugh!"

"Really? I wonder why he asked that? At least he didn't make a run for it! And we've identified two suspects that we can cross off our list – Keelie and Faye, who both have valid alibis." Zaiba looked at her team seriously.

"Who are we focusing on now?" Ali said, balancing on the tips of his toes.

Zaiba turned to Ali and Mariam. "Our main suspects now are the Richards and Connor. I know they were both seen at the play but we can't rule them out. Either party could have snuck out when we were distracted. I also want to investigate Mr Pinel. He was only spotted at the play right at the end and there's something strange about how calm he's been this whole time. It's almost as though he was expecting the crime... Ali, Mariam – I need you to keep an eye on him and the Richards and stop them from leaving the museum. Can you do that?"

"You can count on us!" Mariam said, her eyes showing fiery determination.

"Great."

"But what are you going to do?" Mariam asked.

Zaiba tapped the side of her nose, just like Aunt Fouzia, to let them know that she was in full control but not quite ready to share her full theory. They were closing in on the right suspect, she felt sure of it, and now all that was left to do was locate the teapot. Well, that was *almost* the last thing to do.

First, she needed to talk to someone.

"Poppy and I are going to question Connor now," she said.

Poppy raised her eyebrows. "We are?"

Zaiba nodded. "And you're going to lead the questioning. Use the fact that you like acting as a way in."

Poppy smiled. "Easy peasy."

Zaiba put her hand in the middle of the huddle and, one by one, Poppy, Ali and Mariam added theirs.

"Snow Leopard Detective Agency UK ... let's do this!" Zaiba threw her hand in the air and the others followed suit.

"Let's do this!" they all chorused.

With Ali and Mariam taking their place back in the courtyard, Zaiba and Poppy carefully crossed the small service road and walked to the fenced cliff edge.

"Connor wasn't in the courtyard but I have a hunch where he is," Zaiba told Poppy. They walked down the steps cut into the cliff and into the stands of the open-air theatre. Sure enough, Connor was standing on the stage, script in hand and bellowing out lines.

"I'll turn you in to the customs office and have the money for meself!" he cried to an imaginary actor.

Zaiba and Poppy hopped down the last few steps as quickly as possible. It wasn't until they walked on to the stage that Connor noticed them.

"What are you doing here?" he fumed. "I need quiet and solitude for rehearsal. I'm an artiste!" He put the back of his hand to his brow, as though the mere sight of the two friends caused his artistic soul physical pain.

Poppy took her cue and rushed forward. "Sorry, but I

just *had* to come and ask you about your method!" she gushed. "You see, I want to be an actor too. How do you play your character so believably?" She shook her head in wonderment. Zaiba thought she was a much better actor than Connor!

His face relaxed into a smile. "You have to fully *embrace* the character. I often spend time living as my character. Doing exercises to really embody them like this..."

Connor suddenly started yelling and punching his fists in front of him. "Hai ya! Hai! Hai! HAAAIIIII YAAAAA!"

Goodness! It sounded really frightening but seeing him do it made Zaiba want to laugh and she had to turn round to hide her face.

Hang on! With her back turned, the sound of those shouts reminded her of something. It sounded just like the shouting she'd heard down on the beach coming from inside the cliff! So the shouting *was* Connor after all! The actor was very quickly making his way to the top of her list of suspects.

Zaiba spun round and interrupted Connor's acting exercise. "Connor, if you need privacy, do you ever rehearse somewhere else? Somewhere more ... *hidden?*"

Connor's eyes sparkled and Zaiba got the uneasy feeling he liked playing a smuggler just a *bit* too much. "As it happens, yes. You can access the real-life smugglers' tunnels from the living museum site! Not many people know about it, not even Keelie! I found out about it when I was studying old coastal maps for one of our plays. The acoustics there are simply amazing."

"Where is the entrance to the tunnel?" she asked.

Connor frowned. "I'm not sure I should tell you. It's on a strictly need-to-know basis."

Zaiba thought he *needed to know* a good acting teacher, but she bit her lip and said nothing.

"Why do you ask?" Connor added, looking increasingly suspicious.

Poppy took the lead. "The thing is, we just... We love your work so much, we'd love to see *everywhere* that inspires you. Who knows, when you're really famous, there might be documentaries about these places."

Connor glowed with pride.

Good work, Poppy, Zaiba thought.

"Well, you access the tunnels via one of the corridors in the office block," he admitted. "But don't tell anyone."

Poppy winked. "We won't."

In her mind's eye, Zaiba could see all the clues they'd found swirling around and fitting into place. The missing room... The large painting at the end of the corridor that Mrs Richards had straightened... The crack in the cliff face that opened out to the sea. The criminal must have used the smugglers' tunnel to hide the teapot ... and it might still be there!

Zaiba tugged Poppy's sleeve, pulling her to one side so Connor couldn't hear. "If there's a smugglers' tunnel, the teapot might be stashed there for the criminal to collect later, to avoid suspicion!"

"Like the diamonds on our first-ever mission!" Poppy beamed.

"Connor, where does the tunnel lead to?" Zaiba was speaking so fast, her mouth could hardly catch up with her thoughts.

"You can only access it from the sea at high tide when the water is deep enough to get a boat in."

Tides again! And boats! Zaiba needed to speak to someone who knew the tide patterns of the area well. But for now, she had to work out if they could trust Connor. He would clearly do whatever it took to achieve his goals, but the fact that he'd told them about the tunnels made her think he wasn't the criminal.

"Could you take us to the tunnel from inside the museum?" Zaiba pushed. "Please?"

Poppy painted on her best hopeful face. "I know I could never be as good an actor as you, but maybe if I had somewhere to practise with amazing acoustics I might be a teeny tiny bit as good?"

Zaiba tensed. Had Poppy gone too far with her praise this time?

But Connor's face seemed free of suspicion. "Anything for my adoring fans!"

Poppy and Zaiba jumped up and down. "Thank you, thank you!"

"Let's go get Ali and Mariam. They also love … acting.

Connor, can you meet us by the entrance to the office block? I have someone I need to quickly speak to first." Zaiba was on a roll now.

"No problem, go get your little friends." Connor was clearly still feeling pleased with himself. "Everyone always says I'm great with kids."

Zaiba couldn't help a big smile spreading across her face. They were going to explore a real-life smugglers' tunnel *and* if they were lucky, find the missing teapot!

14
THE SMUGGLERS' TUNNEL

Zaiba checked her watch as she and Poppy raced back up the steps of the clifftop theatre with Connor trailing behind. It was 17:30 already. They were running out of time before the teapot was due to be sent back to Assam!

"Who exactly are we going to speak to *before* we explore the super exciting smugglers' tunnel?" Poppy asked.

"A local expert!" Zaiba grinned, heading back into the courtyard where Ali and Mariam were still in position watching the Richards.

The Richards family were standing in the corner of the courtyard by the café and seemed to be bickering among themselves. Ali and Mariam were behind a bush nearby, hidden if it weren't for their feet, which they hadn't realized were sticking out. Zaiba rubbed her face wearily. So much for secret observations!

"I wonder what they're arguing about?" Poppy said, nodding towards the Richards.

"Whatever it is, Leo is really not happy," Zaiba said. "Look – they're leaving."

The friends watched as Leo strode off out of the museum's front gate. Everyone was supposed to stay *inside* the museum compound! But there was no time to chase after Leo. At least Jacqueline and Sophie were staying put.

"Come on, we need to speak to Faye."

Zaiba and Poppy rushed over to Faye. She had abandoned her protest and was now sitting on her crate, drinking tea.

Zaiba launched straight into her questions. "Faye, living here you must know a lot about the tide patterns, right?"

Faye blinked in surprise. "Oh yes, I've an app on my

phone with the tide tables. It tells you when the tide is low or high, plus there's spring tides and neap tides—"

"Great." Zaiba felt rude for interrupting but time was of the essence. "Could you show me the tide times from yesterday and today?"

"Sure." Faye seemed confused but got the table up on her phone anyway. "Here we go."

Saturday

LOW	04.01
HIGH	10:30
LOW	16.30

Sunday

HIGH	05.18
LOW	11:45
HIGH	17.51
LOW	22.57

"Faye, would you say it's possible to sail a large boat out of the harbour at low tide? For example, if you needed to visit Blacksea Island?" Zaiba asked, noting down the timings of the tides in her notebook.

"Oh no. Our harbour's known for being particularly tricky. The tide has got to be right in for a boat to sail in and out. Makes it pretty tough for the fishing boats!" Faye seemed to be much more cheerful now she was talking about the town. "But where is Blacksea Island?"

Poppy frowned. "It's supposed to be twenty minutes' sail from here."

Faye laughed. "Unless it's an invisible island I think you've got that wrong. I've been to every island around here and never seen any Blacksea Island."

"Thanks so much, Faye. You've been a big help!" Zaiba smiled, putting her notebook away.

Faye blushed. "You're welcome."

They were about to walk away when Zaiba saw Faye's messily written sign dumped on the ground next to her. Something clicked in her mind, and she decided to act on it.

"Faye, are you going to tell Keelie or shall I?" she asked seriously.

"What do you mean?" Faye laughed awkwardly.

"The note," Zaiba said steadily. "I wouldn't want anyone getting the wrong idea."

Poppy gasped and her hands flew to her mouth. All the colour had drained out of Faye's face and she stared at Zaiba hard. "How did you know?"

"No offence, but your handwriting is very messy. In particular, your 'S's look like snakes, and your 'A's are all wonky! At first, we thought it was because the person who wrote the threatening note was trying to hide their identity – but it matches the writing on your sign." Zaiba pointed to the protest sign on the ground. Sure enough, it included lots of wonky 'A's and snaky 'S's. "Then what you said about worrying Keelie couldn't keep the artefact safe and 'wanting to do more', I realized you weren't trying to threaten her with the note, you were warning her. But you really did scare a lot of people."

Faye's eyes filled with tears but she fought them back. "I know. I'm sorry. I just desperately wanted the artefact to stay here and I tried telling Keelie but she wouldn't listen. I was angry and didn't know what else to do, so... I wanted to scare Keelie, but only a little bit.

I was wrong and I'll apologize. But I didn't steal the teapot, I promise!"

"I know you didn't," Zaiba said. "But make sure you apologize to Keelie!"

As they walked away, Poppy tugged on Zaiba's hand. "When did you work out Faye was the one who wrote the note?"

"Sorry, Pops, I only just figured it out when we were talking to her. I guess seeing the messy handwriting was the final jog my mind needed."

"A detective's brain works in mysterious ways..." Poppy shook her head in disbelief. "And what was all that about the tides?"

"I was thinking about how the smugglers got their goods in and out in the past," Zaiba explained. "And I realized our criminals might be planning the same thing. Connor said the smugglers' cave entrance can only be accessed by boat when the tide is right in. That means at high tide. The tide is highest in twenty minutes!"

Zaiba waited for Poppy to put the pieces together.

"You mean, the criminals could be waiting until high tide to sail the teapot out of the tunnels?" Poppy's cheeks were flushed with excitement.

"Exactly. We need to get down there!" Zaiba clicked her fingers. She was about to collect Ali and Mariam when she saw Hassan and Jessica sitting on a bench, looking tired. Ms Talbot and the History Club were nowhere to be seen. Zaiba rushed up to her parents.

"Ms Talbot was given permission to take the rest of the kids back." Hassan gestured in the direction of the B&B.

"Where have you been?" Jessica said, stretching out her arms.

"We're about to crack the case," Zaiba whispered. "But first we need Connor to take us down into the tunnel."

Hassan's eyes grew wide. "A tunnel? Is it safe?"

"He says he goes into it all the time to practise his lines. He seems suspicious, but I really don't think Connor is the criminal. I know it's risky but I think the teapot's down there. I just *have* to look. I'll keep my phone's GPS tracker on the whole time so you can see where we are." Zaiba was speaking so fast she felt out of breath – she had to get her dad to understand. And quickly.

Hassan stayed quiet and looked deep into her eyes. She knew he was thinking of her ammi. But Jessica put a supportive hand on his shoulder and he relaxed just a fraction. "Be careful. If you aren't back here in fifteen minutes, we'll come looking for you. Oh, and ... solve the case, honey," Hassan smiled, stroking Zaiba's cheek.

"I will, Dad. Thank you."

After collecting Ali and Mariam from their not-so-secret hideout, they met Connor in the Great Hall. It was completely empty and with the sun casting long shadows on the walls, it gave Zaiba the creeps. He took them through the doorway that connected the inn building to the office blocks and stopped by the painting, next to the meeting-room door. Once again, Zaiba noticed the worn buttons on the alarm system. There were four numbers that had been rubbed off. A fresh thought started to form in her mind. But before she could concentrate, Connor spoke.

"I bet you don't know where the entrance to the secret tunnel is," he announced, smiling triumphantly.

Zaiba tried not to look too smug as she carefully took the painting down, knocked on the wood, found a hollow spot and pressed, making a panel ping open. Then she swivelled round to see Connor, Ali and Mariam standing open-mouthed, staring at her.

"H-how did you work that out?" Connor gawped.

"I've discovered a secret staircase, a murphy door in a bookcase and a servant's hidden passageway before. Let's just say I have a lot of experience." Zaiba winked.

"Yay! Go, Zaiba!" Poppy cheered, jumping up and down. She gave her friend a big hug.

"Once you told us there was an entrance to the tunnel inside the museum, I put the pieces together. The missing room on the map we saw isn't missing at all. It's faint because it's not a room – it was marking the entrance to a secret tunnel! The painting was hung here to help hide it."

"If you knew where it was all along, why did you ask me?" Connor was irritated.

"I wasn't one hundred per cent sure," Zaiba said. "Plus we need an *expert* who knows the tunnels well to lead the way."

Connor folded his arms across his chest and huffed.

"And we're so excited to see you rehearse!" Poppy said.

Zaiba looked at her best friend with pride. *Poppy, you are a genius!*

Connor puffed out his chest and smiled. "Yeah, you're right. You *do* need me to guide you. OK, follow me."

Zaiba stood aside and let him pass. After all, it seemed dark in the tunnel and she wouldn't want any of her team to slip or hurt themselves. Better he led the way and showed them where it was safe to tread.

The panel slid to the side and revealed a very narrow space in the wall, with a hole in the floor and an iron ladder attached to it. Zaiba gulped.

They really were going underground.

They all lit the torches on their phones and,

carefully, climbed down the ladder until they were below ground level! Once Zaiba hopped off the ladder, she could just about see a tunnel stretching out in front of her.

It was a tight passage, only wide enough that you could stretch your arms out. The walls were made of light grey stone and covered in moss. Zaiba really had to focus on her steps. She stumbled and thought back to the boat trip when she'd had to help Mr Pinel. There's no way he would be able to make it down here, his eyesight was too bad! She was certain he wasn't involved in the theft. In fact, she was sure she knew just what he'd been getting up to.

Zaiba turned on her voice recorder and made a quick note, speaking quietly so Connor wouldn't hear her. "The time is 17:45 hours. We have entered the smugglers' tunnel under the inn. Visibility is poor but we will keep a lookout for the missing artefact." Zaiba switched off the recorder and they carried on walking.

"How did the smugglers make this tunnel without anyone noticing? Seems like it would be noisy to chisel

out all this stone," Ali asked Connor from the back
of the line.

"Yeah, my mum's always complaining about the
builders on our street being too noisy," Mariam added.

"Oh, the smugglers didn't build this. This was
originally a storm drain made for the inn. The rainwater
would run down here rather than flooding the
courtyard." Connor's voice sounded close in the compact
space.

"A storm drain... So the map marked a *storm drain*,
not a tunnel," Zaiba chided herself. "Of course, no one
would mark a secret tunnel on a map for everyone to
see!"

"OK, here we go," Connor called back to them.
Zaiba noticed the tunnel had opened up into a large
space. It was a stone cave, with a floor made of mud
and shingle. There was rubble and large rocks strewn
about on the floor and even an old glass lamp screwed
into the wall. Someone from the original inn must
have installed it. Connor lit the candle and it cast a
dim yellow hue.

"Everyone, look in these rocks," Zaiba instructed. "The teapot could be stashed here!"

"Teapot? I thought we were smugglin' gold!" Connor suddenly bellowed in his One-Eyed Jack character voice.

Zaiba remembered they'd brought Connor down here pretending they were interested in his acting. He wanted to give them an acting lesson!

"Right, of course." She tried to mimic his accent. "Erm ... everyone on the lookout! Find the gold."

"Yessir, Captain." Poppy saluted, immediately getting into the swing of it.

"Yeah... Aye, aye." Mariam wasn't so sure.

The team set to work, carefully rolling over large stones and even digging through the shingle to find anything that might be a historical artefact, stashed away for safe-keeping. Ali emerged from behind a large chalk stone holding two dusty bits of cloth.

"It's not a teapot, Cap'n, but I found these here ... hats?" He was doing his best smuggler's voice and Zaiba had to repress a laugh. Given the serious situation, now was not the time to get the giggles!

Connor noticed what Ali was holding, "Those aren't no hats, they're bonnets! The barmaids up in the inn wear 'em."

Zaiba took the bonnets and stowed them away in her backpack. Anything found down here could be evidence and she had a feeling that she knew why these bonnets were down here. She scanned the cave and saw an opening that looked like another tunnel leading down into the cliff face.

"Where does that go, yonder?" she asked Connor, pointing at the dark tunnel, still trying to act like a smuggler.

"Why, that's the access tunnel, Cap'n! Opens out into a big cave at sea level. When the tide is high our men can sail a boat right into it."

"And out of it..." Zaiba narrowed her eyes. "Does the cave look like a big crack in the cliff face, with lots of pointy rocks jutting out of the surf ... uh, mate?" Zaiba was quickly getting tired of the smugglers' act, but at least it was keeping Connor happy.

"Aye, Cap'n – that's the one. You seen it?" Connor

asked, pretending to search for a bundle of gold.

"I saw it in the distance when we were exploring the beach but I couldn't reach it."

Zaiba thought back to the tide tables. High tide was soon, they didn't have much time. She looked at Poppy, Ali and Mariam all scrabbling and searching on the ground. Her mind flashed back to something she'd read in *The Cottage on the Cliff.* Something not written by Eden Lockett...

As she listened to the roar of the tide coming in, Zaiba slipped off her backpack and retrieved the book. She flipped through the pages as quickly as possible, shining her phone light on the words. She was looking for something her ammi had written in the margin...

There!

Keep your feet firmly on the ground, but your head looking up to the sky!

Zaiba snapped the book shut. "Mates, look *up*! Maybe we'll find the treasure hidden up high!"

Everyone shone their lights on the walls of the cave.

Connor tutted. "Smugglers of the seventeenth century

didn't have phones, you know. This is *not* very authentic. When you're acting, you really need to stay in character."

Zaiba tuned him out, sweeping her light around every nook until...

"I see something!" she called. There was a dip in the wall of the rock about six metres up. Could it be a hole? "One-Eyed Jack, can you give me a lift?"

"Aye, aye." Zaiba had to admit that Connor was very good at staying in character. He hoisted Zaiba up on to his shoulders and she reached into the dip.

"I can feel something."

"Please don't be a spider," Ali whimpered.

"Come on, Zaiba, you can do it!" Mariam called out.

Zaiba reached in as far as she could and felt her fingers brush against a parcel. She gripped the packaging, which felt like bubble wrap, and pulled it towards her. It was a large, circular package, tightly wrapped in plastic. She passed it to Poppy as Connor placed her down, a shocked expression on his face.

"Is it the teapot?" Zaiba gushed, looking at Poppy.

They shone the light on it. Through the packaging,

they could just make out the shine of gold!

"It's the teapot!" Poppy sang, holding on to it tightly.

"Wait, you were searching for that all this time?" Connor said. "You're not fans after all!"

He looked so hurt that Zaiba couldn't help feeling a stab of sympathy for him. "Sorry we had to lie to you, Connor. Sometimes you have to keep secrets to yourself when you're in the middle of an investigation. But it *was* fun acting as smugglers with you, and look – we've got the teapot! And look... We found gold!"

Connor hesitated, before his face split into a grin. "And I helped!"

"Not *that* much," Mariam muttered, but Poppy quickly shushed her.

Zaiba's mind was still whirring. They'd found the teapot. Good – but now they needed to catch the culprit. Or, in this case, culprits...

Suddenly, the sound of people approaching made everyone freeze in place.

It was the criminals ... and they were heading right for them!

15
CAUGHT IN THE ACT!

"The boat should be here in ten minutes if we've timed it correctly," a voice said. Zaiba recognized it immediately. It was Jacqueline Richards! And she was coming this way.

Zaiba put her finger to her lips and silently instructed everyone to hide behind the largest rocks in the cave, but not before she'd snuffed out the lamp. Once she was safely crouched in her hiding place, she started recording a video on her phone.

"You should have let me do it, I'm the better sailor in the rowboat." Sophie's voice was much closer.

"Leo will do just fine. Have more faith in them," Jacqueline scolded. "We'll go down to the cave first and guide Leo in before we retrieve the teapot."

"Are you sure Leo will be safe?" Sophie sounded nervous. "There are all those rocks by the cave mouth, and they seemed angry when they left."

So that's where Leo went to when they stormed off, Zaiba thought. They'd gone to sail the small rowboat into the sea cave at the bottom of the tunnel!

The voices were right next to them now. They were all in the cave together! Zaiba's heart was pounding so hard she was amazed the sound wasn't bouncing off the rocks and around the tunnels. Next to her, Mariam shuffled slightly in her crouched position. Zaiba held her breath. Mariam was not as experienced as her, Ali and Poppy – they needed to be completely quiet! But the Richards family clearly hadn't heard anything.

"As long as Leo has us guiding them in, they'll be fine," Jacqueline said. "A few rocks aren't going to stop us. This teapot is too important. With a piece like that, we'll be revered among all collectors. With this and the rest of the collection we've acquired, our family will become legendary!"

"Not that we'll be able to show it to anyone," Sophie retorted. "Or the rest of the gold tea set we've gathered. Everyone would know they're stolen."

"Give it a few years and all this hubbub will have died down, it always does." Jacqueline's voice came quieter now. They'd passed through the last tunnel and were heading to the cave at the bottom where Leo would be waiting to be guided in.

Zaiba stopped recording. "Come on, let's go," she whispered.

With Connor once again leading the way and Zaiba holding on to the teapot, the team made their way back up the tunnel, being careful not to be spotted by the Richards. As one by one they climbed the iron ladder up to the meeting room, Ali finally spoke. "So it was the Richards all along?"

"The kids seemed nice," Poppy tutted.

"I think their mum made them do it," Zaiba said, hauling herself up the ladder last.

"Imagine your mum making you a criminal." Mariam extended a hand and pulled Zaiba up into the corridor.

"That. Was. Amazing," Connor gushed. "If I knew how exciting being a detective could be, I'd have added it to my acting repertoire years ago."

Zaiba turned round and clicked the panel back into place.

"What now, Zai?" Poppy looked at her friend intently.

"The police must be here by now," Zaiba said. "We have the stolen teapot and the criminals responsible trapped in this tunnel. They've only got two options of escape. Back up the way they came, or out of the cave by boat. They're using the rowboat because it's small enough to get through the narrow passage into the tunnels, but it's not big enough to hold all of them. They'll need to come back up to the museum and then head to their family boat to leave. Connor, go and find the police and tell them to send some officers to the Richards' boat in the harbour immediately. Wherever they go, we'll catch them!"

Poppy smiled and Ali and Mariam nodded in agreement. Still reeling from the events, Connor rushed off to fetch the police. He had obviously forgotten that his smuggler character would never be caught *dead* helping the authorities. But this wasn't acting, this was real life.

And they were about to catch the criminals!

Keelie and the security guards led two police officers, a man and a woman, into the corridor where Zaiba and her team were waiting. Keelie looked very embarrassed to still be in this situation and Jo and Tom were refusing to look at each other. Zaiba worried that they hadn't made up from their falling-out, but hoped they'd forgive each other soon. Making up after a fight makes a team stronger!

But right at this moment, there were bigger details at hand.

"Zaiba?" the male police officer said. "Tom here says you're the person to talk to about this case." He reached out to shake Zaiba's hand and, a little surprised, she took it, keeping her grip nice and firm. Her dad always said you could tell the character of a person from their

handshake, and Hassan knew almost everything!
Though not as much as Aunt Fouzia, obviously.

"Yes, I'll fill you in," she said, taking out her notebook.
"But we'll have to be quick. First things first, did you send
someone to the Richards' boat?"

The female police officer nodded. "We sent one of the
team who came with us down to the harbour. They'll be
stationed at the boat any moment."

"Good." Zaiba glanced at the time on her phone: 18:05.

Hopefully the Richards would head back up to the
corridor through the secret entrance once they realized
the teapot was missing.

Talking at about a hundred words per second, Zaiba
told the police *everything*. "The Richards are antique
collectors. They live on Blacksea Island – at least they say
they do. I think it's a false location they've given so they're
less easy to track. They also have access to a rowing boat
and knowledge about the tides. They have a collection of
antique maps of the coast, and I overheard Ms Richards
talking to Keelie about the smugglers' tunnels, so she
must have known about this one. They came to the play

so they'd have an alibi. I remembered seeing them there because they have such distinctive looks and Jacqueline caused a scene about popcorn to make sure everyone could place them at the play. But they were sitting right at the back – one or more of them could have easily snuck out and in again during the performance while everyone was distracted. We found *these* bonnets down in the tunnels. They were probably used to hide their distinctive hair colour and blend in with the staff while sneaking out. That's why no one noticed them leave."

"But why hide the teapot at all? Why not just leave immediately?" the male police officer said.

Zaiba grinned. "I thought that too. But when I saw the tide charts for yesterday it made sense." She pulled out her notebook and read from the table. "Saturday 16:30 LOW. The tide was low when we were watching the play, so they couldn't sail the teapot out of the cave then. They had to choose a time when the tide was high, plus everyone who was at the play was due to attend the reveal the next day. It would have looked too suspicious if they sailed home straight after the play."

"Jacqueline's a good actress." Poppy shook her head. "I really believed she was upset about the teapot going missing."

The male officer was thinking. "The museum director here claims she locked the door with an alarm code. Any idea how the Richards got past that without setting it off?"

Keelie looked at Zaiba with wide eyes, obviously desperate for answers. Zaiba winced. She hadn't had time to fully think this through yet, but she would have to do it on the spot. "The alarm system Keelie is using is old. Well, old enough that some of the numbers on the keypad have been rubbed off from use. Four numbers. The four numbers of the security code, I'm guessing. I bet the safe had the same combination, too."

Poppy leaned over to the meeting room door and looked at the keypad, reading out the numbers that had been rubbed off. "One ... three ... four ... eight."

The police looked at Keelie expectedly and she nodded grimly. "I'm terrible at remembering codes so always just use the same numbers."

"The Richards siblings must have heard Faye complaining about how Keelie always uses the same passwords and they love number patterns and puzzles," Zaiba rushed on. "We saw them doing a puzzle book outside. Once they had the four numbers, they just had to try all the different combinations. Am I right, Ali?"

Ali counted on his fingers. "With those four digits there are twenty-four possible combinations."

"So one of the Richards kids snuck over to the museum during the play and caused a banging sound at the back office entrance to draw the security guards away. Then they came in, figured out the keycode and stole the teapot from the safe, locking it and the door behind them so they didn't arouse suspicion, while their mum stayed at the show as an alibi. I'm figuring one of them must have changed the CCTV when they were in the office block too, to erase any trace of them coming or going. Then they stashed the teapot down in the smugglers' cave and got back to the play, where Jacqueline had stayed to give them an alibi." Zaiba took a deep breath and Ali whistled.

"Criminals are bad and everything but ... that's impressive," he said.

Finally, Zaiba pulled out her phone. "And if you still don't believe me after all that, I have a video of them talking about the teapot and a rowboat about ten minutes ago down in that cave."

"The teapot!" Keelie exclaimed as if coming to her senses. She came forward and gently took the parcel from Zaiba's hands. "I want to check it's the real thing."

The police officers nodded for her to go on. After all, if it wasn't the real deal, then all this was for nothing.

Keelie extracted a pair of white gloves from a drawer in a wooden cabinet near the door. Gently, she peeled off the layers of bubble wrap that had been wound round the parcel. As she pulled them away, Zaiba watched in awe as a beautiful gold teapot emerged! It was small, with a round oval body and a long, thin spout. The handle was a dark ebony wood and even though it was slightly tarnished, Zaiba could still make out the engravings of Asian elephants.

It was the most beautiful teapot Zaiba had ever seen.

Keelie stepped back and appraised the object. She turned it over carefully and looked at the logo stamped on the bottom. "This is the real thing."

Zaiba smiled. *You certainly can tell a lot from a logo!* she thought.

The police officers said nothing for a moment. The female police officer had been taking down notes the whole time and only now, once Keelie finished speaking, did she look up.

"Amazing work, Zaiba. But where are the criminals?"

The sound of muffled voices behind the sliding panel answered that question.

"You're about to meet them," Zaiba whispered.

From behind the panel Zaiba could hear Jacqueline's strained voice. "I'm not leaving without that teapot!"

Then the painting moved to the side and Jacqueline's head appeared. Her face was bright red and her hair dishevelled, probably from frantically searching the cavern in the tunnels. When she spotted the police, she immediately tried to duck behind it.

"Just a minute," the male officer called. "We need to talk to you."

Jacqueline slowly climbed out into the corridor, followed by Sophie and Leo, who'd both gone very pale indeed.

"I was just showing my children the historical tunnels," Jacqueline lied. "Such an educational experience."

Zaiba stepped forward and gestured to the teapot in Keelie's hands. Jacqueline's eyes nearly popped out of her head and she made a move to grab it but Zaiba stepped in front of her. Immediately, Jacqueline's face flushed and she hid her hands behind her back. She just hadn't been able to help herself!

Tom and Jo shared a knowing glance. That had been one big giveaway.

"Just checking out the tunnels?" Zaiba said. "So, this stolen teapot ... we wouldn't find your fingerprints all over it?"

"The teapot! O-of course not." Jacqueline shook her head.

"And we wouldn't find your rowboat docked down in

the *secret* smugglers' cave, where the teapot was stashed, ready to be taken away?" Zaiba pressed on.

This time Jacqueline remained silent. Zaiba knew she had to bring out the big guns to get her to confess.

"Well, Ms Richards, if you don't want to speak now, I suppose we could just listen to this video of you down in the tunnels talking about your plan to steal the teapot." Zaiba flicked on her phone and started playing the recording. There were gasps from Keelie, the Sikoras and the Richards children.

As soon as she heard the sound of her voice, Jacqueline started shaking. When she heard Sophie's voice she burst into tears.

"The children have nothing to do with it. I forced Sophie to crack the alarm codes for me and scrub the CCTV!" she cried out, hugging Sophie and Leo to her. They were both sobbing loudly too.

Jacqueline was led away, with her children following behind, heads hanging low. As she passed Keelie, the museum director shook her head. "History isn't to be hidden away in private collections. It belongs to the people," she said, her eyes blazing.

Once the police had gone, Keelie turned to Zaiba. "I can't thank the Snow Leopard Detective Agency UK branch enough. You saved the teapot *and* possibly my job! The council will be so pleased to hear we found the teapot with as little press attention as possible. It's all down to you."

Keelie put her hand out and Zaiba shook it firmly, feeling very professional indeed. "It's our pleasure, Keelie. But could you promise me something? Once Faye has made a *very important* apology to you, could you forgive her and perhaps give her a job here at the museum? She could be an expert of the local area. That way she would feel more involved with the museum and preserving Chesil Bay's heritage. She would realize that the town doesn't need to keep hold of foreign artefacts."

Keelie thought about this idea for a moment, looking at Zaiba. "That sounds like a good idea. I'll see what I can do. Now I'm going to take this teapot and get it shipped!"

As she hurried out, Zaiba could not stop smiling.

The thief had been caught. The artefact was safe and would soon be where it belonged. And she'd finally got the chance to see the beautiful teapot in all its glory! Aunt Fouzia would love it – such drama over a pot of chai!

16
IT'S OFFICIAL

Once Keelie had left the room, carrying the teapot as carefully as the Crown Jewels, the friends started chatting excitedly about what had happened. But they were interrupted by the sound of clapping coming from the doorway to the Great Hall. Zaiba turned round to see Christophe Pinel, slowly applauding her.

"Well done, Zaiba," he said, smiling.

"Why are you so pleased?" Poppy said, stepping forward protectively.

"Yeah, you've been acting weird this whole time!" Ali agreed, holding his sister's hand.

Zaiba squeezed his hand and chuckled. "It's OK, guys.

I know who he is."

"You do?" Mariam gawped.

"He's Aunt Fouzia's friend! I finally recognized him by his laugh. Aunt Fouzia said you snorted when you laughed. You were much younger in the photo she showed me but you still look the same." Zaiba suddenly blushed. "Not that you look old now..."

Christophe laughed, snorting again in the way Aunt Fouzia remembered so fondly. "You really are a brilliant detective, mademoiselle. As soon as you mentioned the Snow Leopard Detective Agency I knew who *you* were too. I have been acting strangely, I must admit. You see, I was here to investigate a gang who have been stealing artefacts from museums for a while now, so I was expecting the teapot to go missing too. I wanted to intercept the criminals."

"You mean the Richards *have* stolen before?" Zaiba shook her head. "They did mention down in the tunnels that the teapot would complete their set..."

"Oh yes, I think most of their collection is stolen. But no one has been able to catch them before.

Not even me. You children have made me realize it might be time to retire. My sight is no longer as sharp as it was, and I keep missing things... Like that faintly drawn room on the map you saw."

"I still have some questions," Ali said, stepping forward. "Like, where were you during the play? And how come you didn't help us when you realized we were investigating too?"

Christophe blushed ever so slightly. "I apologize if I came across as rude. During the play I was scoping out the museum entrance, thinking the criminals would have to leave through it with the teapot. But I was in completely the wrong place."

"You were," Zaiba chuckled. "Sophie Richards was at the back of the office block banging on the wall to get the security guards to come out."

"But how could they possibly know that both Tom and Jo would leave their post?" Poppy scratched her head.

"They didn't. I guess we'll never know what they would have done if Connor's vocal warm-ups hadn't drawn Jo away as well."

Christophe looked at Zaiba admiringly. "You're just as smart as your mama, you know."

Zaiba's heart skipped a beat. "Did you know my ammi?"

"Oh yes. I worked with her and your aunt a number of times when their investigations brought them to France. Just before she went on maternity leave, she came to see me to say goodbye." Suddenly Christophe's face clouded over. "I am so very sorry that she disappeared like that."

Zaiba felt Poppy, Ali and Mariam surround her tightly. Tears pricked at her eyes, but she knew that she was never alone, not with her friends and family around her.

"You are the future of detecting, Zaiba and the Snow Leopard Detective Agency," Christophe announced. "I know that your ammi would be so very proud of you."

Gathering in the lobby of the B&B, Zaiba and the History Club looked out at the view of the sea for the last time. After a final night in Chesil Bay, it was time to go home. Nobody wanted to leave – especially not Ali! He was currently clinging on to Khushi tightly, wrapping his arms round her skirt.

"I want to live here forever!" he cried, trying to hold back tears. "How can I cope without your curry?"

Khushi stroked his head fondly. "You can come back whenever you want. Besides, you are local heroes now for finding the teapot!"

"And heroes of Assam too," Anil said, putting his palms at his chest in a namaste position. "Thank you, Zaiba. I heard the artefact was shipped off safely after the police inspected it."

Ms Talbot called from outside. The bus was there to take them to the train station! Now the whole History Club rushed over to the Duttas to squish them in a hug.

"Hey, hey, no more tears," Hassan said, trying to usher the kids outside. "It isn't goodbye forever."

"Just goodbye for now," Khushi finished the sentence.

After a few more tearful goodbyes from Zaiba, Poppy and Mariam, the Duttas waved off the History Club and Chesil Bay faded from view.

The train journey home was slightly less exciting than on the way there. After all, coming *back* from holiday was never as much fun. But Jessica had brought colouring books and pens to cheer the kids up and Hassan was testing out some of his dad jokes.

Zaiba, Poppy, Ali and Mariam were once again engaged in a tense game of Snap when Ms Talbot came over to Zaiba's seat. She crouched down beside her in the aisle, her multicoloured scarf wrapped round her shoulders.

"Zaiba, I want to apologize for not believing you about the teapot." Ms Talbot kept her eyes lowered. "As your teacher, I should have encouraged you but I got swept away in the competition. History isn't about winning. It's about uncovering the truth – and you certainly did that and more."

"Thank you, Ms Talbot." Zaiba smiled at her. Then she

raised her voice slightly. "History Club, let's give three cheers to Ms Talbot for the best trip ever!"

"Hip hip, hooray!"

"Hip hip, hooray!"

"Hip hip, hooray!"

Ms Talbot stood up and accepted her applause by curtseying dramatically. "How about we go to the Sherlock Holmes Museum on our next trip?" she said to the carriage, and everyone responded with more cheers.

Just then, Zaiba heard her dad calling to her from the seats behind. "Zaiba, answer your phone! Aunt Fouzia said she's been trying to call you."

Fumbling in her backpack, Zaiba retrieved her phone and pressed the accept button. Poppy was sitting next to her, and she craned her head to look too. Aunt Fouzia's beaming face popped up on the screen and Zaiba felt her own smile mirror her auntie's.

"Sweeties! I can't believe you've done it again. The Snow Leopard Detective Agency UK branch just has success after success." Aunt Fouzia blew kisses at the camera.

"Thanks, Auntie. I couldn't have done it without Poppy, Ali and Mariam."

Aunt Fouzia nodded. "Of course, a detective is only as good as their team."

"And guess what, I met Christophe Pinel!"

Aunt Fouzia's eyes looked like they might pop out of her head. Zaiba was over the moon – it was so rare she could surprise her auntie!

"What? He's still working? I must get in touch with him..."

"Poor Christophe," Hassan called. Zaiba looked back to tell her dad off for teasing and he winked at her.

All of a sudden, there was a blood-curdling scream from behind Aunt Fouzia on screen.

"What's that?" Poppy cried.

"Auntie, is something wrong?" Zaiba panicked.

"It's just the baby!" Another face came appeared on the screen – it was Samirah, Zaiba's cousin. In her arms, she was bouncing a chubby baby with thick dark brown hair. Baby Nabiha!

"Oh my gosh, who knew babies were so loud?"

Mariam said, covering her ears.

"I thought there had been a murder!" Ali agreed.

Samirah laughed and jiggled Nabiha around.
The baby gradually stopped crying and started
giggling instead, which made Poppy and Zaiba
giggle too!

"Being a mum is a tough job," Sam said, wiping
up some drool from the baby's mouth. "But I love it.
Though I'm hoping I can go back to my other job soon."
Sam was a doctor, a brilliant one at that, and Zaiba
knew she'd been missing her career since having the
baby. Zaiba thought of her own ammi, going back out
into the field only a year after she'd had Zaiba.

"I'm sure you'll be back on the wards in no time,"
Jessica added from her seat. "I got back to work pretty
soon after having Ali."

"Do you think my ammi wanted to go back to
work too after she had me?" Zaiba asked Aunt Fouzia.
"She had to get back to detecting?"

"Oh, definitely." Aunt Fouzia smiled. "She loved
detecting as well as being a mum. And if she hadn't

gone back out on that last case and sent vital evidence back to our headquarters, we never would have caught that horrible man and the forest would have been destroyed."

Zaiba's heart leaped in her chest. "So, you mean she cracked the case?"

"She always did." Aunt Fouzia smiled warmly. "Just like you did. She would be so proud of you, Zaiba. Your legacy as a detective is the crimes you've solved."

"Yes!" Ali announced dramatically. "Everyone will always remember the great Agent Zaiba who solved the case of the missing diamonds."

"And the summer fete poisoning!" Mariam added.

"*And* the haunted house," Poppy joined in.

"And now, a stolen priceless artefact from a smugglers' shipwreck." Aunt Fouzia grinned. "In fact…"

Aunt Fouzia reached down and pulled her Scrapbook of Legends into view. She opened the last page and there, pasted next to a picture of her ammi, was a new picture. One of Zaiba!

"Agent Zaiba, you are officially a legend," Aunt Fouzia

announced. "Right next to your ammi, the legendary Agent Nabiha."

Poppy gave Zaiba a big hug, "You deserve it, Zai. You're the best detective ever."

Zaiba felt happy tears stream down her cheeks and she quickly wiped them away. Hassan got up from his chair and leaned all the way over the seat to kiss Zaiba on the head.

"My daughter is a legend!" he announced to the carriage and everyone cheered.

Zaiba laughed and pretended to bow in her seat. She was a real detective, and not just that, *a legendary one* just like her ammi!

"Thank you, Aunt Fouzia." She beamed. "But you know, I'm still just getting started! It's like Eden Lockett's golden rule number one says: *Stay ready. Mystery is always around the corner.*"

And Zaiba knew she'd always be there to find it.

DO YOU HAVE WHAT IT TAKES
TO JOIN ZAIBA AND THE SNOW
LEOPARD DETECTIVE AGENCY?

TURN THE PAGE
TO FIND OUT!

EDEN LOCKETT'S GOLDEN RULES

1. Stay ready. Mystery is always around the corner.

2. All good detectives make notes.

3. A good detective weighs up all the options.

4. Use every sense available to you. Touch, sound, taste, smell and sight.

5. A good agent always ensures the safety of their friends.

6. When you have to cover a lot of ground, split up and spread out.

7. Snacks are a detective's best friend. Samosas are the best!

8. Be kind – you never know someone's secret.

9. Don't be afraid to ask for help!

10. A great leader inspires by example.

11. The best agent is cool, calm and oozes charm.

12. Always ask why.

13. Revealing your findings before the crime has been solved can hinder the investigation!

14. Mirrors come in useful in all sorts of ways...

15. Take note of everything around you. The smallest detail could be the biggest clue!

EDEN LOCKETT

THE COTTAGE ON THE CLIFF BY EDEN LOCKETT

EXCLUSIVE EXTRACT

The wind whipped hair across my face as I ran down the stone steps leading to the beach. I'd ditched the eyepatch in the cottage but I was still wearing the pantaloons, which billowed around my legs.

Not ideal. But there'd been no time to get changed after returning from the rehearsal and being a detective often did involve doing slightly odd things, such as chasing a suspected thief across a beach dressed like a pirate.

"Eden Lockett, you are never going undercover again," I muttered to myself. But I knew that wasn't true. It was one of the most fascinating parts of being a detective.

And at least this time I'd only been pretending to be an actor in a local theatre group!

I kept my eyes on the flash of scarlet up ahead, as I splashed through rockpools and dodged children building sandcastles.

Finally, I stopped beside a boat shed. There was a trail of footsteps leading towards the door. The wearer of the red cape was clearly inside.

A musty smell wafted up my nostrils as I opened the door, and a strange snuffling sound reached my ears. That didn't sound human!

A pale, terrified face popped out from behind one of the boats.

"It's OK," I said gently.

The girl shuffled out into the light. It was Alice, the daughter of Ms Bright, the owner of the bookshop on the promenade.

"I saw you leaving the cottage as I was arriving," I said. "Are you the one who's been stealing things from around the village? Mr Tenby's watch, Mrs Dixon's gloves, and the rest?"

Alice shook her head vigorously.

There was that sound again! I recognized that noise – and it definitely wasn't human.

"There's a dog here, isn't there?" I said.

Alice reached behind the nearest boat and brought out a gorgeously fluffy puppy!

"She's a stray," Alice explained as the puppy licked her face. "I was scared Mum wouldn't let me keep her so she's been staying here. But she keeps getting out. And she also keeps..."

Alice paused. The puppy was now nibbling her glasses like she was trying to tug them off.

"Stealing things?" I suggested.

Alice gasped.

"And you were trying to put it right," I continued. "That's why you were in the cottage when I came back from the theatre. You were putting back Mrs Dixon's gloves!"

"They're a bit chewed now," Alice said, blushing. "I know Mrs Dixon always leaves the door key underneath the plant pot, and that she and you would be at rehearsals."

"I thought the thief was one of the theatre group members. It was mostly their stuff that was going missing," I said.

"At first, I kept the puppy in one of the dusty rooms at the back of the theatre but the caretaker almost caught her," Alice explained. "That's when I put her here, instead. I didn't realize she'd stolen things until later, I promise! She'd stuffed them down the back of the little bed I got her."

I smiled. "I believe you. And I think if you asked your mum about keeping her you might be surprised at the answer." I'd been in the bookshop yesterday and seen Ms Bright stroking a customer's spaniel. I could tell she was a bit nervous around dogs but she'd been smiling too.

"I'll ask her. And I'll return the rest of the stolen things," Alice said.

"What's the puppy's name?" I asked.

Alice chewed her lip. "I can't decide."

"You can use one of my favourite names if you like.

If I ever have a daughter, this is what I'm going to call her."

Alice smiled. "What is it?"

"Zaiba," I said.

THE SECRETS OF SMUGGLERS

Smuggling started in the late thirteenth century. It began as a result of a payment, known as a customs duty, that was placed on wool. At first these payments were small, but over time governments increased them whenever they needed to raise more funds. When taxes were raised, there was more smuggling and more violence.

During the eighteenth century, there was huge growth in illegal trade on England's coast. Smuggling became an industry as the customs duties started to include more items. Enormous quantities of goods — including tea and alcohol — were being smuggled into England. It wasn't until the 1840s, when a free-trade policy reduced import duties, that smuggling stopped being an option.

The term 'smuggler' covers lots of different people. From the sea smugglers, who used their knowledge of sailing and navigation to make some money when times were tough, to the men on land who waited for the cargo and brought it on land. Another key role was that of the tubmen, who carried the goods away from the coast. In some communities, everybody would have been involved! To be successful in smuggling, strength in numbers was key.

Smugglers would bring the contraband back to Britain in small ships with sails. They would make their way to the coast, where their companions would be waiting. The timing had to be precise, and communication was essential to make sure the goods could be brought to land and the smugglers avoided capture.

HISTORY IS MORE THAN JUST FACTS!

As Zaiba and the History Club learn, there's more to history than just learning facts and dates! It's about the people who lived through it, their experiences and how they differed. We also need to learn from history, and to do that we need to think carefully about what we're told.

When we're taught history, it's important to remember that it's presented through the lens of whoever is telling it. History is recorded by those in charge, the people with the power. That means that we are only seeing one side of the story: we're only learning about one person or group of people's experiences. Keep in mind when reading a report who the writer is, and  what we know about them. Context is key to fully understanding the facts.

As well as analyzing about the information we're given, it can be as interesting to think about what's missing from records. Then we can seek out other accounts, reported by sources from different backgrounds that can give us a more rounded view of what happened.

History is fascinating – there are an infinite amount of things to study. And we're all part of it! If you're like Zaiba and on the look out for a mystery, perhaps pick a person or a place that you're interested in, and read up on them. You could start with someone you know! Talk to them about their past and research into the stories they tell you. You never know what you'll find! You could even create your own Scrapbook of Legends...

SCRAPBOOK OF LEGENDS

Create your own Scrapbook of Legends!

Pick two people who inspire you and make a note of why.

Legend: _____

What are they like? _____

_____

_____

_____

_____

Favourite memory: _____

_____

_____

_____

_____

Legend: _____

What are they like? _____
_____
_____
_____
_____

Favourite memory: _____
_____
_____
_____
_____

ACKNOWLEDGEMENTS

Writing these four books has been a delight and a privilege. *Agent Zaiba Investigates* was the first book I had published, back in February 2020 just before lockdown hit. I'm so grateful for the messages readers, teachers, librarians and parents have sent me via social media to let me know how the books have been received out in the world. I hope to meet more of you in real life in the future!

These books wouldn't have been possible without Karen Ball at Speckled Pen. Thank you for your amazing notes, detailed plans and support for me as a new author. I appreciate it so much!

To my wonderful agent Davinia Andrew-Lynch, for always having my back – thank you for ever.

A big thank you to Daniela Sosa whose charming and gorgeous illustrations have made this series so special.

And finally, a massive thank you to all the team at Little Tiger. The whole process has been so lovely from start to finish. A special thank you to my amazing editor, Mattie Whitehead, who has put so much work into this series, including multiple tricky mystery planning sessions. I can't thank you enough for all your contributions.

I hope people keep reading and re-reading Zaiba's stories and enjoy her mystery solving as much as I enjoyed writing it. Snow Leopard Detective Agency for ever!

Annabelle Sami

ABOUT THE AUTHOR

Annabelle Sami is a writer and performer.
She grew up next to the sea on the south coast of the
UK and moved to London, where she now lives, for
university. At Queen Mary University she had an amazing
time studying English Literature and Drama, finally
graduating with an MA in English Literature.

When she isn't writing she enjoys playing saxophone
in a band with her friends, performing live art
and swimming in the sea!

ABOUT THE ILLUSTRATOR

Originally from Romania, Daniela Sosa now lives and works in Cambridge with her husband and is completing an MA in children's book illustration at the Cambridge School of Art.

Creating a magical mix of the ordinary and the unusual, Daniela enjoys highlighting subtle detail and finding beauty in everyday life. She gets inspiration from nature, books and observing the world around her.

COLLECT THEM ALL!

ANNABELLE SAMI — ILLUSTRATED BY DANIELA SOSA

Agent Zaiba INVESTIGATES

THE MISSING DIAMONDS

ANNABELLE SAMI — ILLUSTRATED BY DANIELA SOSA

Agent Zaiba INVESTIGATES

THE POISON PLOT

ANNABELLE SAMI — ILLUSTRATED BY DANIELA SOSA

Agent Zaiba INVESTIGATES

THE HAUNTED HOUSE

ANNABELLE SAMI — ILLUSTRATED BY DANIELA SOSA

Agent Zaiba INVESTIGATES

THE SMUGGLER'S SECRET